If It Hadn't Been for Yoon Jun

Marie G. Lee

Houghton Mifflin Company
Boston 1993

Printed in the United States of America
BP   10   9   8   7   6   5   4   3   2   1

Library of Congress Cataloging-in-Publication Data

Lee, Marie G.
   If it hadn't been for Yoon Jun / Marie G. Lee.
      p.   cm.
   Summary: As she reluctantly becomes friends with Yoon Jun, a new
student from Korea, seventh grader Alice Larsen becomes more
interested in learning about her own Korean background.
   ISBN 0-395-62941-1
   [1. Identity — Fiction.   2. Korean Americans — Fiction.
3. Adoption — Fiction.   4. Schools — Fiction.]   I. Title.
PZ7.L5138If   1993   92-9557
[Fic] — dc20   CIP
                             AC

To Karl

ACKNOWLEDGMENTS

Many thanks to all the people who shared their stories with me or otherwise helped me with my research, especially Grace K. Lee, Mom and Executive Director of the Minnesota Korean-American Multi-Service Center; Ann-Marie Trost; and all the parents who are bringing up Korean-American children in loving homes.

And, as always, *muchas gracias* to Wendy and Laura.

If It Hadn't Been for Yoon Jun

Chapter 1

❀ ❀ ❀

The day came too soon, and yet not really soon enough for Alice Larsen.

She and her friend Minna had tried out for the seventh-grade cheerleading squad — and the cheerleaders were going to be announced today.

In school.

In front of everyone.

At breakfast, Alice couldn't eat a single bite, so she decided to go to school early.

When she got there, she found that Minna and their other best friend, Laura, were already there, at the locker the threesome shared.

"We couldn't stay home either!" admitted Minna.

"Don't feel bad if you don't make it — they're harder on seventh graders because they think they can just try out again next year," said Laura. As the school's ace reporter and brain, she always tried to look at things from every angle. Even though she herself hadn't tried out, she was every bit as nervous as Alice and Minna.

"But they've never had seventh-graders as good as we are try out," said Minna, some of her usual confidence returning.

"You'll make it at least, Minna," said Alice, who tried to act as though she didn't care.

The three girls all had health class first period with old Miss Hendricks. Since the beginning of the year Miss Hendricks had separated them into three different corners of the room because she said they were such "chatterboxes." Today they went in early, continuing to talk loudly to each other from their seats.

At 8:05 on the dot, the principal came on the school's intercom, blowing into the microphone to get everyone's attention.

"Good morning, boys and girls. I'd like to start off the announcements by informing you of a change in the school lunch menu."

"Come on already!" pleaded Minna. Miss Hendricks shot her a frown.

"Instead of sloppy joes on Wednesday, tuna casserole will be served. Repeat: tuna casserole will be the main dish for Wednesday's lunch. The next item of business is that Miss Brant, the cheerleading coach, and Mr. Verant, the director of P.E., would like to announce this year's Bainer Junior High cheerleaders . . ."

2

Alice looked at Minna, who gave her the thumbs-up sign. Laura smiled encouragingly.

"Carolyn Olson, Janet Prince, Jody Carlson, Minna Lund, and Alice Larsen will be on the squad."

Minna made it! was Alice's first thought.

HEY, I MADE IT!! was her second.

"Hooray!!" Minna said, throwing up her arms. Laura looked as if she was going to burst with pride.

"Congratulations, girls," Miss Hendricks said nicely. "Now, it's time to concentrate on our anatomy lesson."

Anatomy! Alice thought. Who could concentrate on anatomy when the most wonderful three minutes of her life had just passed? She and Minna had practiced cheers until they both thought their arms would drop off, but she had never dared hope that both she and one of her best friends would make the Bainer Junior High cheerleading squad!

Chapter 2

❀ ❀ ❀

"I made cheerleading!" Alice hollered when she got home.

"Oh Alice," said her mother, "I'm so proud of you!"

"You're a real cheerleader?" asked her fifth-grade sister, Mary, her eyes wide with awe.

"Yup," said Alice. "Minna made it, too."

"That's absolutely wonderful," Mrs. Larsen said, taking the Saran Wrap off a plate of chocolate chip cookies. She laid the cookies next to the pitcher of milk sitting on the kitchen table. Then she gave Alice a big hug.

"Did I tell you that I was a cheerleader at Bainer Junior High, too?"

"No, you didn't," Alice said, surprised. "What was it like?"

"I can remember the day I got picked," she said. "I was absolutely thrilled. Cheering the games was lots of

4

fun, and there were a lot of nice boys on the team. I might have even dated one or two of them."

"Mom! You dated in junior high?" Alice couldn't imagine her mother, who was always holding hands with her father, even thinking any other boys were cute.

Her mother corrected herself. "Not really *dated*. Just getting sodas together and stuff like that."

"Hmm," Alice said. She, Laura, and Minna had been finding all sorts of excuses to walk by football practice after school, and there was actually this seventh grader on the team, Troy Hill, who she thought was really cute.

"Oh, not to change the subject," Mrs. Larsen said, "but I meant to tell you that Mrs. Johnsrude, the lady from the Lutheran Adoption Services Agency, called today to let us know that a Korean family is going to move up to Bainer."

"Does this have something to do with Camp Kimchee or something?" Alice asked, a little uneasily.

"Well, you know how Mrs. Johnsrude thinks the camp is a good idea," Mrs. Larsen went on. "She also thought that meeting the Korean family would be a good way for you to start to learn about Korean culture."

Alice knew Mrs. Johnsrude only as some lady in Minneapolis who occasionally sent her these fliers for a Korean culture camp that they held every summer up north for Korean adoptees. Even though her mother and father had encouraged her to go — it was only for a week — she just wasn't interested, and her parents said the decision was hers.

"I already told her I'm not interested in Korea," Alice said firmly. She didn't like to think of herself as being adopted, period. It made her feel funny, especially when some people called Mary the "real" daughter, as though being from Korea made her, Alice, a fake.

"I know I *look* Korean," Alice went on, taking a bite out of a cookie, "but I don't feel Korean at all. I feel totally American, like you and Dad and Mary."

"That's good, honey," Mrs. Larsen said gently, then added, "Mrs. Johnsrude was just trying to help."

"I know," Alice said. She tried to sound agreeable, although she couldn't possibly like some lady whose sole purpose in life seemed to be to remind her that she was adopted.

"We'll wait until the family actually moves in before we figure out what we're going to do," Mrs. Larsen said. "I just thought you'd like to know."

"Thanks, Mom," Alice said, as she and her little blonde-haired sister continued to munch on the chocolate chip cookies. She couldn't wait until her father came home so she could tell him about cheerleading.

Chapter 3

❀ ❀ ❀

After school the next day, Alice and Minna went to the gym for their first cheerleading meeting. All the other girls were already there, giggling and talking a mile a minute.

Alice and Minna felt a little shy, since they were the only seventh graders. The other girls looked so much bigger, and wiser.

"Hi, you two." One of the eighth graders had come up to them. Alice remembered her from tryouts as the girl who could do perfect back handsprings.

"I'm Janet Prince," the girl went on. "But you can call me Dusty — all my friends do."

"Dusty," said Alice. She liked that. The girl had beautiful brown hair that was streaked blonde from the sun — exactly the kind of hair Alice would like to have if she wasn't stuck with straight black hair.

"I'm Minna," said Minna, remembering her manners. "And this is Alice."

Dusty smiled. She seemed to glow.

"Hi, Minna and Alice," she said. Then she walked away to join the rest of the eighth graders.

"Hello, girls," said Miss Brant, the coach. "And congratulations. You all know what an honor it is to be picked as a cheerleader for Bainer Junior High, so I expect you to strive to be good examples for the other students."

All the girls nodded solemnly.

Then Miss Brant handed out the blue sweaters and skirts that Alice had been yearning for ever since sixth grade, when she, Minna, and Laura had started going to junior high football games.

"Oh dear," Miss Brant said, when it was Alice's turn. "You're so tiny! I hope this small size will fit."

"I can roll up the sleeves," Alice said quickly. She ate and ate, but always stayed the same, eighty-six pounds. It was a bother sometimes, being so small. Her little sister Mary was already gaining on her in height.

"That's good for us, though," Dusty Prince suddenly spoke up. "We'll need someone small to do the 'other team will fall' cheer."

She was talking about the cheer where the smallest girl stands on top of the biggest cheerleader's shoulders. Then, while they chant "The other team will fall," the girl on top literally falls, and the other cheerleaders catch her.

Alice looked over at Dusty gratefully.

Miss Brant gave each girl one blue and one white

pom-pom. They would practice twice a week starting Thursday, and the eighth graders who'd been on the team last year would teach them everything they knew.

"I can't wait," Minna whispered to Alice, squeezing Alice's arm.

"Me either," said Alice. "This is going to be the best year!"

Chapter 4

❀ ❀ ❀

It was Saturday, which meant it was mall day. Alice, Laura, and Minna spent most Saturdays hanging out at the mall. It was the place to see and be seen, especially in the winter, when, in Minnesota, it got too cold to do much else.

Today, they had an official mission: to go to J.C. Penney's to get cheerleading saddle shoes for Alice and Minna.

Alice's mom drove them there in the Larsen family's Jeep Wagoneer, the same one they'd use to bring Mary and Alice to church school in the morning.

After being dropped off, the three girls walked toward the entrance of the Hematite Mall. Alice wanted to faint: Troy Hill — from the football team — and his friends were just ahead of them.

"Hey there," he said, opening the door for her. "You're Alice Larsen, right?"

"Yes, thanks," Alice said, going through the door. "And you're — uh — Troy, right?" Of course she knew he was Troy Hill, but she didn't want him to know that she secretly looked for him at football practice.

"Yeah," he said. "I'm Troy Hill."

Alice heard some of his friends chuckling behind her.

"I think he likes you," whispered Laura as they made their way toward Penney's.

"No kidding," said Minna, less quietly. "Isn't he the cutest, Alice?"

"I guess so," Alice said. To tell the truth, she thought Troy was really cute, and nice, and everything. She'd just never really known any boys — except for Minna's little brother, who was only nine. And even though she and Minna and Laura talked about boys all the time, none of them had any firsthand experience. This was one of the things about junior high that made them nervous and excited.

"Try talking to him," Minna suggested. "I would."

"That's because you're a flirt," Alice said, poking her friend in the side.

At Penney's, the two girls ordered blue-and-white saddle shoes from the catalog. That took about two seconds. They decided to cruise the mall. Alice hoped she'd run into Troy again.

By the big fountain with the colored lights under it, they saw Dusty Prince. She was with a girl whom Alice had remembered seeing around school. The girl was Indian. Her name was Julie Grayhorse or something like that. There were only about five Indian kids in the whole junior high, and they pretty much all hung around together; some of them were known to cause trouble. Alice couldn't figure out what Dusty Prince, a *cheerleader,* was doing with this girl.

"Hi, Dusty," Minna said, proud to be using her nickname.

"Hi, guys," Dusty said to all of them. "Do you know my friend, Julie Graywolf?"

"Hi, I'm Alice," Alice said to the girl, who was lighting a cigarette. Alice couldn't believe that Dusty Prince would hang around with someone who smoked!

"Hi," the girl said back. She pushed her lank hair out of her face and puffed away at her cigarette.

"We just ordered our saddle shoes at Penney's," Minna said to Dusty.

"Oh! I should get mine today," Dusty said. "I hope I have enough money with me." She searched her pockets.

"You could put it on my mom's card and pay me back," Minna said helpfully. Dusty's eyes lit up.

"You're great," she said, and then she turned to Julie.

"I'm going to run over to Penney's with Minna. Want to come with?"

"Nah, I'll go get some more smokes," Julie said, looking over at Alice and Laura as if they should be impressed.

Laura and Alice told Minna they'd sit by the fountain for a while.

"I don't know why a cheerleader like Dusty Prince would want to hang around with someone like that," Laura said, once they were gone. "Did you see how she was smoking?"

"It was hard to miss," Alice agreed.

"I've heard that Indian kids are bad news," Laura went on. "Whenever I stay after school for the paper, they're always the ones I see in detention."

Alice shuddered a little. The Indian kids really stood out in school, with their dark hair and dark skin in a place where a lot of the kids were very blond and white-skinned. It made her think that maybe she looked weird and out of place in school, too. After all, she was the only person who had black-black hair and almond-shaped eyes.

"Laura, do you think I look weird?" Alice asked, suddenly. Laura looked at her as though she thought Alice was joking.

"No, why would you think that?"

"Oh, nothing," Alice said, but inside, she felt secretly relieved.

Chapter 5

❀ ❀ ❀

Alice, Laura, and Minna were sitting at their usual lunch table when Troy Hill came up to them. He sat down next to Alice. She could feel herself blushing, despite her promise to herself to act cool.

"Hi," he said.

"Hi," she said.

"Did you have fun at the mall?"

"Yeah."

"How's cheerleading?"

"Oh, fine."

"How's football, Troy?" Minna interjected, as the conversation seemed to need livening up.

"Pretty good," he said. "I made the first cut at least."

"Oh, you'll make it," Alice found herself saying. In practice, he ran like a cat, and he always caught the ball, no matter how poorly it was thrown.

"Thanks," he said, smiling at her. Alice's heart skipped — just a little.

"Anyway, the other guys are saving me a seat. See ya."

"See ya," the three girls chorused.

Alice watched Troy walk away to another corner of the lunchroom. He was really neat. She wished she wouldn't get so tongue-tied around him.

"You have to be more energetic about talking to him," Minna advised, "or he won't be able to figure out that you like him."

"I agree," said Laura.

"I never know what to say," Alice groaned.

"Who's that?" said Minna suddenly, pointing to the bench by the cafeteria door, where no one ever sat.

"Who?" said Alice and Laura.

"That kid, sitting by himself over there — I've never seen him before."

Sitting a little to the side of the empty table was a fat kid with short, spiky black hair, and, Alice thought, pimples. He was eating with his head down, shoveling in UFOs — unidentified food objects — as fast as he could.

He also had, she noted, eyes like hers.

"Must be a new kid," said Alice. "I've never seen him before."

"Ugh," said Laura. "I hate watching obese people eat."

"Do you guys have any idea who he is?" asked Alice.

"No," said Minna.

"No, me neither," said Laura.

"Oh well, we'll find out soon enough," Minna said, looking first at the new kid, and then at Alice.

Alice had a sudden realization that made her heart sink: it had to have something to do with that new Korean family her mother was telling her about. It would be just her luck that they would have a kid and the kid would be in her grade.

Chapter 6

❀ ❀ ❀

On Wednesday, Alice and Minna walked into their homeroom and saw the new kid in there.

Mrs. Choquette, their homeroom teacher, ushered him to the front of the room the way she always did for all the new students. He stared at the floor.

"This is Yoon Jun Lee from Seoul, Korea," she said.

"He's a June Goon?" yelled Travis Jones, the class bully, from the back of the room.

A few kids snickered. Alice felt her face grow hot. She didn't want to have anything to do with a country that gave its people such strange names.

"Mr. Jones, please raise your hand next time," Mrs. Choquette said crisply. "And his name is *Yoon Jun Lee.*"

She wrote it on the blackboard in large letters.

"I want you to make sure you pronounce it correctly," she said and smiled at the rest of the class. "Let's all give Yoon Jun a big Bainer Junior High welcome."

The class clapped politely and pretty loudly. Yoon Jun continued to stare at the floor. Today, Alice noticed, he was wearing glasses, and he really did have little red pimples all over his face — she thought you couldn't get acne until you were at least thirteen.

Minna and Alice looked at each other and shrugged.

"Maybe there's something wrong with him," Alice whispered. "Like he's special ed or something."

Minna stared at him one more time as Mrs. Choquette ushered him back to his seat.

"Hey, you're Korean, aren't you, Alice?" Minna said suddenly.

Alice's mouth went dry, like sandpaper, for a second. "No," she said quickly. "I'm not really. I'm not the same kind — I'm American."

Her friend looked at her with a hint of question still left in her eyes, but by then the bell was ringing, and it was time to go to class.

Chapter 7

❀ ❀ ❀

That Friday night, Alice, Minna, and Laura went to the senior high school football game. Alice liked seeing the high school cheerleaders in action.

"At the last junior high game, I saw Dusty Prince do that split jump where you touch your toes in the air," said Laura, who now liked Dusty as much as the other two did. Dusty occasionally sat with them at lunch — but she always brought her friend Julie along with her.

"Dusty is great," Minna said.

"I don't see why she hangs around with Julie Graywolf when she could be so popular if she wanted to," Alice said without thinking. "Oh oh, that sounded horrible, didn't it?"

"Well, I see what you mean," Laura said. "Julie Graywolf is so — I don't know."

The words, "ugly" and "weird" were on the tips of their tongues, but no one said it. Alice had often romanticized the Indians when she was younger. They were a noble people who lived off the land, wore great feathered headdresses, and soft buckskin moccasins. But when she looked at Julie Graywolf, or any of the other Indian kids who slouched in the halls looking as if they didn't care about being in school, she didn't see any of that. She only saw their lank hair, dull skin — and cigarettes.

Alice was sure Dusty didn't smoke — cheerleaders weren't allowed to — but why would she hang around with someone who did? It was tough to figure out. But despite all that, Alice still thought Dusty was wonderful.

After the game, the three girls happened to run into Troy, who was with his friends from football, Peter Kemp and Dean Jacobs. Three and three. Pete, who sometimes wrote sports stories for the school paper, smiled at Laura, Alice noticed. Maybe Dean would start liking Minna.

"Feel like going to Country Kitchen?" suggested Troy.

Alice looked at her friends. Laura and Minna nodded in agreement.

"Sure," Alice said.

Chapter 8

❋ ❋ ❋

Country Kitchen was just across the highway from the high school football field. Troy took Alice's elbow and hurried her across the dark stretch of road. There were car lights in the distance, but the other four made it safely, too.

The Country Kitchen sign buzzed and flickered unsteadily as they walked under it. During the day it was just a one-toothed boy with a bumblebee on his toe, but at night, the orange neon made the boy seem to have an evil smile; it made Alice, Laura, and Minna even more afraid to cross the highway, but they always wanted to go, because Country Kitchen was a high school hangout, and it made them feel grown-up.

Alice dove into one of the orange vinyl booths and Troy followed her. Pete went on the other side. Laura looked at him a little uncertainly, but then slid in with him. Minna sat next to Alice, and Dean sat across from her.

Everyone giggled nervously.

They ordered plates of fried mushrooms, french fries, and pops — diet Pepsis for the girls and Cokes for the boys. Troy plunked a quarter into the jukebox that they had at their table.

"You can choose the first one," he said to Alice.

Alice reached over him and turned the dial to view the selections. Country western was definitely out, as was heavy metal. She wanted something quieter, but not mushy. She settled on a classic, "Sunnyside Days."

Troy let Minna and Laura each pick a song. Minna picked Sid the Killer's "Flies of Summer," and Laura went for the more sedate "The Cat's Whiskers" by Stevie Oaktree.

Alice felt Troy's foot touch hers under the table. Was it just a mistake? It stayed lightly on top of hers. She'd heard of something called "playing footsie," but she wasn't sure if this was it, or how to play back. She looked at Troy and smiled instead. Laura and Pete, she noticed, were deep into a conversation on the best way of interviewing people for an article.

Their food came, crispy and piping hot. The boys descended on it like starving puppies, but Alice wasn't all that hungry. She sat back and sipped her pop.

At the other end of the restaurant, she saw someone who looked familiar. It took her a second to connect the hulking form in a soiled busboy's uniform to Bainer Junior High, but then she realized it was that new kid, Yoon Jun Lee.

"Psst." Alice nudged Minna and caught Laura's

eye. "Look over there." She motioned with her eyes.

"Isn't that the kid in our homeroom — the one with the funny name?" asked Minna.

"What's he doing, working here?" said Laura.

"I don't know," Alice said. "I guess he's a busboy."

"Who's a busboy?" asked Troy.

Alice motioned again with her eyes. Yoon Jun Lee had his back to them.

"That kid. He's in our homeroom."

"I think I've seen him around. What's his name?"

"Yoon Jun Lee — or something like that," Alice said. "He's new."

"Hmm," said Troy. His face had a funny expression as he stared at Yoon Jun Lee.

This made Alice uneasy. Was he thinking that Yoon Jun Lee was weird-looking, and if so, did that mean he thought *she* was weird-looking?

Dean slurped the last of his Coke noisily through his straw. "That felt good," he said. Alice almost expected him to burp next.

He did — *blaap!*

"Say excuse me, you slob," said Troy. Alice was glad that he wasn't looking at Yoon Jun anymore.

"Excuse me," Dean said.

Their table was a mess. It was time to ask for the bill. The sooner, the better, Alice decided. Just being in the same place as Yoon Jun Lee was making her nervous.

Pete plunked another quarter into the jukebox and

punched in some songs. Alice's heart sank. Now, they had to wait until the songs were finished.

Alice felt Troy's hand reach for hers under the table. She caught her breath. It was the first time she'd ever held hands with him — with anybody. Well, maybe hanging around a few minutes more wouldn't be so bad. His hand was nice and warm. She hoped hers wasn't sticky or greasy or anything like that. She'd been using Jergen's lotion every night in anticipation of this great event.

Alice heard a clanking noise, and all of a sudden there was a dish cart parked in front of their table, and all six of them were staring at the new kid, Yoon Jun Lee.

He looked scared of them. His eyes behind his glasses were wide and unsteady. Quickly, he began grabbing the ketchup-smeared plates, and he threw them on the ones already perilously stacked on his cart. Then he jerked his hand out to get a glass, and he spilled a little water that had melted from the leftover ice onto Laura. He looked like he was going to cry when he saw what he'd done.

"So sorry," he said, shakily. It came out like "so sallee."

Laura looked horrified, but she managed to say, "That's okay."

He fumblingly grabbed the rest of the dishes, pausing every so often to push his glasses up his nose. Then he hurried the cart away.

"What a klutz," said Pete, surveying the splashes on the front of Laura's sweatshirt. He politely handed her some napkins.

"Alice, is that your cousin or something?" asked Dean. From the look on his face, Alice could see he wasn't joking.

"No!"

Minna turned and glared at Dean. "That's a dumb question," she said.

"Well, they're both, you know, Asian," said Dean.

"Alice is different — she's American," Minna said firmly.

"Well, I didn't know," he said pleadingly to Minna. Alice thought he did look really sorry.

And Alice was feeling sorry for herself. What if the whole school thought they were related? She would just die.

Chapter 9

❋   ❋   ❋

"So, Alice," said her father at dinner. "Have we got a surprise for you!"

"Really? What is it?" she asked. Her birthday was still months away.

"We're going to have you meet a *Korean* family on Wednesday. They have a nice boy named Yoon Jun who's in your grade."

"Ooh," groaned Alice. This couldn't be happening. "You didn't. Tell me you didn't."

"Why, I thought you'd be thrilled," her father said, surprised.

"Mom," Alice said. "I thought you said we could wait until they moved in and *then* decide what to do."

"I did say that, dear," she answered apologetically. "But your father found them first."

Alice wondered if it had something to do with church. Her father was the minister at the First Lutheran, and he always got excited when he heard of new people moving to Bainer.

"Let's say that they found me," Reverend Larsen said cheerfully. "Mrs. Lee and Yoon Jun were Presbyterians in Korea, but there aren't any Presbyterian churches in Bainer, so they're interested in finding out more about the Lutheran church, and I invited them for dinner on Wednesday."

"Fine!" Alice was surprised to hear herself almost shouting. "I'll eat dinner at Laura or Minna's house that night while you and Mom talk to them about church."

"Now Alice," her mother said gently. "We also thought this might be a good time for you to learn a little bit about Korea."

"Why?" Alice said.

"Because it's a part of you," said her father.

Alice sighed. She must have had this conversation with her parents about a hundred times — no, maybe a million. If they thought her reasons for not wanting to go to Camp Kimchee were okay, why should they think she would want to meet a Korean family, much less one where the kid seemed to be a complete dork?

"Look, maybe you don't understand." Alice decided to take another tack. "I already know who he is in school, and I'm not friends with him, and no one I'm friends with is friends with him either. It's not a normal thing to invite people like that to dinner."

"Alice," said her father disapprovingly, "where is your Christian spirit of welcoming strangers into your home? And remember, if not for the kindness of other Christians, you wouldn't be here."

Alice shut her eyes. She hated it when he brought that up. It was as if he could blackmail her in a way that he couldn't do to Mary just because she wasn't their "real" kid.

Alice looked over at her mother. Her mother at least knew what it was like to be in junior high, to be a cheerleader, and to be popular.

"Mom," she said, low, "the kid is a real dweeb. I don't want to eat dinner with him. Please, please can we skip this?"

"Okay dear," her mother said quietly. "Let's see what we can do."

* * *

Alice had been hearing the low hum of her parents' voices coming out of their bedroom, and once, she clearly heard her name.

She knew it was wrong, but she just had to hear what they were talking about. She pressed a glass to her bedroom wall. She had seen someone do this in a movie once, and she was surprised to find that it worked — it was as though she had a private ear into her parents' room, which was right next door.

"I'm telling you, our daughter is happy as she is without our foisting a foreign culture on her," her mother was saying.

"A lot of kids don't like what's unfamiliar," her father replied. "She ought to at least give this family a chance. I talked to the mother the other day — an extremely nice woman — and she mentioned that her son was a bit lonely in school. It's not easy coming to a school in Bainer, where the kids have all been together for years and are very tight with each other. I thought perhaps Alice could become friends with the boy and learn a little about her culture on the way."

"What do you mean, *her* culture?" said her mother. "She's my — our daughter."

"But Karen, you know where she comes from."

"Her biological mother gave her up. I think that gives us the right to bring her up as our own, as an American."

"It doesn't change the fact that she's of Korean ancestry," said her father.

"But I thought the whole reason that we went to the Lutheran agency was so we could take a poor little thing out of a third world country and give her the best America has to offer. Look, she's made cheerleading — she seems to be fitting in fine without any help from her Korean past."

"She's old enough that we can start showing her both sides of the coin," said her father. "We owe it to her."

Her mother didn't say anything.

"Look, can we just try it?" said her father. "Please bear with me, your overzealous, do-good husband. And remember what the woman at the adoption service agency said — that most of these adopted Korean kids eventually do become curious about their Asian heritage."

"Is that what she said? That orientation meeting was so long ago."

"She did say that. And besides, what could it hurt?"

Alice removed the glass from the wall. It could hurt plenty. Why couldn't her parents talk to her like a human being and take her own feelings into account? Did it ever occur to them that she might already have an opinion about this Korean boy, Yoon Jun Lee?

If she had kids, she would never think of forcing them to be friends with someone just because they were American or Korean or anything.

Chapter 10

❋ ❋ ❋

It was final. That morning at breakfast, her mother told her that they had to have dinner with the Koreans. Her mother said that she was sorry, but the plans had already been made, and the Lees would be very, very disappointed if they didn't get to meet her. Alice wanted to disappear into a hole in the ground. What would her friends think, having that weird kid over for dinner?

She decided to tell them right away, to make sure they were clear on the fact that she had absolutely nothing to do with it.

"Parents just have the wackiest ideas, don't they?" she said to Minna and Laura at lunch.

Laura glanced over at Yoon Jun Lee, who was there, like a fixture, at the table near the door. "Well," she said, "he might have some interesting stories to tell — he's from a whole different country."

"I guess," Alice said, unenthusiastically. She

couldn't imagine that boy with the pimples saying anything she'd want to hear.

"And it *is* Korea," said Minna. "Like, do you ever think about, you know, your real parents?"

Alice felt like cold water had been splashed in her face. "Mom and Dad *are* my real parents," she said. "As far as I'm concerned."

"I mean your Korean parents," said Minna.

"The Korean part would make an interesting story," said Laura. "Do you have any memories of Korea?"

"What story?" Alice said, a little loudly. A few heads at the next table turned.

"I have a mom and dad who've raised me since I was a baby," Alice lowered her voice a notch. "And they love me — is that so unusual?"

"Sorry," Laura murmured. "I didn't mean anything by it."

"I guess it is kind of dorky," said Minna, a little apologetically. "You don't even know this kid and here your parents are hauling him over for dinner."

"Exactly," said Alice. "And they expect me to talk to him and be friends with him and stuff — ugh!"

"I wonder if he eats regular food," said Minna. "Isn't Korea where they eat cats?"

"I don't know," said Alice. She wasn't even too sure she knew where Korea was on the map. "We're serving roast beef."

"You can tell him it's cat," said Minna. "I can cut

32

off some whiskers from Muffin, and you can put them on top of his food, like parsley."

Alice couldn't help smiling.

"You are so gross, Minna Lund," she said.

"Call us the minute he leaves," Laura insisted.

"I will, I will," Alice said, wishing it were already over.

*　*　*

"Okay, it wasn't as bad as I thought it'd be," Alice said to Minna, over the phone. She'd flipped a coin to see which friend she should call first, and Minna won.

"That kid came over with his mother. I guess he doesn't have a father. They really didn't say much. His mom asked Dad a few questions about church, and that was about it — they didn't tell me much stuff about Korea, after all that."

"What did they tell you?"

"Oh, how Seoul, that's the capital, is so big and how there are mountains all over the place. Pretty boring stuff. She asked me if I could speak Korean, and of course I said no. What a silly question — where would I learn it? She had an awfully funny accent, too."

"What about the Yoon Jun kid? What was he like?"

"Minna, he was exactly the same way he is at lunch every day. He just sat there and looked at his food the whole time. He didn't even look up when we were introduced."

"Geez," said Minna. "I wonder what's wrong with him."

"You know what else?" Alice said. "Koreans can't drink milk — isn't that weird?"

"What do you mean? Everyone's got to drink milk."

"Not everyone," Alice said triumphantly. "When Mom gave him a glass of milk — you know how I always have milk with dinner — "

"Me too," said Minna.

"His mom said he couldn't drink it because he's milk *intolerant*."

"That sounds serious."

"She said a lot of Koreans are. See, I drink milk fine. I'm not the same."

"Oh sure, you're American, after all, like Laura and me," Minna said. "Anyway, why didn't *he* tell you all this?"

"I'm serious, he didn't say two words," Alice said.

"Anything else?"

"Oh yeah, his mother brought this dessert thing that she said was rice balls with bean powder."

"Rice *balls?* With bean powder?" Alice could hear Minna hooting practically from the other side of town.

"Yeah, I told Mom that I was too full. Mary took a bite, though, and she said it was totally gross. Mom had to finish it."

"Sounds gross. Aren't you glad that's over with?"

"Oh yeah," Alice said. "Mom even said I shouldn't

feel any pressure to be friends with him or anything.
And Minna?"

"What?"

"Would you please not mention this to anyone? I'll
tell Laura, and then just you guys will know."

"Of course," said Minna. "If my parents had Yoon
Jun Lee over for dinner, I guess I wouldn't want to be
advertising it all over the place, either."

"Thanks, Minna. I'll call Laura now."

"See you in school tomorrow."

Chapter 11

❀ ❀ ❀

The next day, Alice glanced nervously over at the table near the lunchroom door, afraid that Yoon Jun Lee might suddenly decide that he should sit with her just because he'd had dinner at her house.

Alice sat down with Minna and Laura at their usual table, and she couldn't believe what she saw: on the table's surface, someone had drawn, with pencil, a big messy heart that said "Yoon Jun Lee loves Alice Larsen."

"Ooh," she moaned to Laura and Minna, "look at this."

"Do you think it was Yoon Jun who did this?" asked Minna.

"Who else?" said Alice. She glared at his table. Amazingly, he was sitting there, exactly as usual, hunched over his food.

"Let's get this off," said Laura. They didn't have any erasers with them, so Minna tried using spit on the table's polished, plastic-like surface. It worked reasonably well, and the other two joined in, spitting discreetly into their hands and rubbing their fingers on the offensive scrawl.

"The nerve of him," Minna mumbled. "He must have thought your parents were trying to arrange a marriage for you two at dinner."

"That's not funny," Alice groaned. She wouldn't put it past her father to give Yoon Jun the impression that it was *she* who wanted to have dinner with him — just to make him feel like less of a loser or something.

"Maybe we should tell the principal," said Minna. "Graffiti is against school rules, right?"

"Maybe this is some bizarre Korean custom," suggested Laura. "Like he's thanking you for dinner."

"Whatever it is, I don't like it," Alice fumed. She didn't know what to do. Her father had made her promise that she would try to be nice to Yoon Jun. Did the promise count if he was going to do things like writing on cafeteria tables?

"Are you going to say something to him?" asked Minna.

"I don't know," she said. "I promised my father that I'd try to be nice to him."

"Well, live and let live," said Laura. "Besides, the big football game against Arkin is today — you have more important things to worry about."

* * *

37

"Go, Troy, go!" Alice screamed.

Troy had the ball, and he was streaking toward the goalposts.

"T–D, T–D," the cheerleaders chanted. Alice waved her pom-poms furiously, hoping her exertion could give Troy extra speed.

An Arkin guy leaped to clobber Troy, but he ended up only grabbing Troy's ankle. Troy shook him off like a dog and sprinted home.

"Yay!" squealed the cheerleaders, in one voice.

"Yay!" cheered the fans, including Laura.

"All right, Troy!" yelled Alice.

Dusty Prince smiled at her and gave her a big hug. "Your boyfriend just won the game for us."

"He's not my boyfriend," Alice said modestly.

"Not *yet,*" said Dusty. To Alice, Dusty looked amazingly tall and beautiful in her cheerleading sweater and skirt. She probably didn't need all sorts of pins to hold the outfit in place, as Alice did.

After the game, Alice waited to congratulate Troy. Minna and Laura, winking, said they had to get home. Troy came out the door, his hair still wet, cheeks pink. He broke into a smile when he saw Alice.

"Hey," he said.

"Hey, great game," said Alice. She wanted to hug him.

"Thanks," he said. "Thanks for cheering for us — it really helped."

Alice didn't know what to say next.

"Cat got your tongue?" he asked.

"Uh," said Alice.

Troy laughed. "I guess so. How about a milkshake at Country Kitchen?"

"Sure," said Alice. She was walking on a cloud. Stepping on cotton candy. Floating.

Over a chocolate-banana shake, Alice decided that Troy looked even cuter up close. "You know," she said, finding it somehow easier to talk when they were also engaged in sharing a straw, "when that Arkin guy tackled you, it sort of looked like he was a dumb dog that you shook off your leg."

Troy laughed. "I thought the exact same thing," he said. "I even pretended I was a postman, and I had to run away from the dog to deliver the mail."

Alice envisioned Troy as a mailman in blue, the football his letter bag, and the Arkin player a dog chewing at his ankles, and she laughed, too.

"Neither rain nor sleet nor an Arkin defensive player . . ." said Alice.

Troy cracked up. "You're funny," he said.

Alice couldn't have been happier.

Chapter 12

❀ ❀ ❀

Alice, Minna, and Laura couldn't believe it.

Dusty Prince had been suspended from school because she'd gotten into a fight.

Laura had been there. It happened after school, and she had been on her way to the newspaper. What she had seen was Travis Jones, the school bully, teasing Julie Graywolf. Everyone knew that Travis Jones was bad news. In elementary school, he used to steal milk money from the younger kids. In sixth grade, the ASPCA was after him because they'd suspected him of shooting a litter of puppies with a BB gun.

According to Laura, he'd been pretending to do an Indian war dance, hopping around on one foot, patting his mouth with his hand and going "Whoo-whoo-whoo-whoo — how! Ugh!" Julie Graywolf, who normally looked so tough, seemed about to cry.

Then Dusty had arrived on the scene.

"I think she said to Travis, 'Shut your trap, you jerk.' "

"Sounds like Dusty," Alice concurred admiringly.

"And so Travis said back, 'Why are you defending an Indian *bitch?*' "

"Then what happened?" asked Minna.

"Dusty started beating him up — socko! Wham! He didn't have a chance."

"She got suspended for beating up the class bully?"

"I guess the principal blamed her for starting it all," Laura said sadly. "I gave her my eyewitness testimony, but Travis was on the floor bawling like a moose."

"What a baby!" exploded Minna. "And what a horrible thing to be teasing Julie about — she can't help being Indian."

"Do you remember," said Alice, "last year when Travis Jones called me a 'Chink'? At least Mrs. Swenson made him apologize to me in front of the whole class."

"And didn't he make a federal case about it — the teacher being so unfair to him?" said Minna. "As if he gave any thought to *your* feelings."

Alice was feeling sorry for Julie Graywolf. Travis hadn't teased *her* since then, but she still remembered how bad it had felt. It must be worse for Julie, since other kids — not just Travis — made it clear that they didn't like the Indian kids. They *were* an odd group, she admitted; a lot of them seemed to come to school just to cut classes, hang out in the halls, and smoke. But it was a free country, right? Her father kept saying that it was better for them than being on reservations.

"I think Travis Jones might have problems at home," said Laura. "Not that it excuses him or anything. I heard that his father was in Vietnam and that he's been sort of wacko ever since. Did you ever notice how Travis's hair is always cut in that short buzz cut? I head someone say something about it to him, and he said, 'My old man wants it that way — and what my old man wants, he gets.' "

"Ugh," said Alice. "I'd rather not think about Travis Jones's life. I'd rather think of something constructive, like coming up with a way to help Dusty — I hope she doesn't get kicked off cheerleading."

"Yeah," said Minna. "We have to do something to help her."

Chapter 13

❀ ❀ ❀

For the first time, the *Bainer Bugle* ran an editorial. It was written by its star reporter, Laura Kristiansen, and titled FREE DUSTY (Janet) PRINCE! It read as follows:

On October 23, I saw what I think can be called a "miscarriage of justice."

One Travis Jones was teasing a fellow student in a way that was both mean and rude. Dusty (Janet) Prince came along and told him to stop harassing her friend.

Jones told her off, including calling her friend an "expletive deleted."

Miss Prince, like any friend, tried to convince Jones of his wrongdoing by physically hitting him, when nothing else seemed to work.

Although this incident happened on school property, it was after school hours, and anyway, Miss Prince was just doing what any good friend would do. If anyone should have been suspended, it should have been Jones.

Let's bail Dusty out of jail. No more suspension, I say!

"I don't remember Travis calling Julie an 'expletive deleted,' " said Alice, as she read the article. "That sounds like too big a word for his vocabulary."

"No, 'expletive deleted' means a swear word has been taken out. I substituted it for 'Indian bitch.' "

"I'm surprised the principal let you print this," Minna said.

"She almost didn't," Laura said. "But you know, I saw something on TV about the freedom of the press — specifically in editorials. It said all I had to do was be clear that I was expressing an opinion. She agreed, in the end."

"Way to go, Laura!" Alice said, proud of her friend.

"I only hope it'll help Dusty," Laura replied.

Alice was a little worried. What if they kicked Dusty off cheerleading? It wouldn't be the same without her.

The three girls looked at each other solemnly.

* * *

Dusty came back to school early the next week, but it was hard to tell if the editorial had helped get her back any sooner.

Miss Brant said Dusty would be barred from cheering two games because, as she said, "even if Dusty was

44

fighting for a good cause, cheerleaders are still repre-
sentatives of the school, and fighting is against school
rules."

Alice didn't quite agree, but she was overwhelmed
with relief that Dusty would be back. Dusty even
came, quite diligently, to the practices that week.

"I think you did the right thing," Alice whispered
to her, when they stood together, getting ready to
practice the next cheer.

"Thanks," she said. "I do, too."

"Dusty, would you like to come to the mall with
Minna, Laura, and me on Saturday?"

Dusty thought for a minute. "Sure," she said. "Can
I bring Julie along?"

"Sure," said Alice. Whatever Dusty wanted was
okay with her.

Chapter 14

❀ ❀ ❀

On Saturday, Laura's mom drove the five girls to the mall. Dusty had called Mrs. Kristiansen beforehand to give directions to her house, since her address was listed as a "rural route" in the phone book, which didn't tell anybody anything. Julie would be at her house to make the pickup easier.

"To tell you the truth, I've never been out this way," said Mrs. Kristiansen as they crossed over the railroad tracks where the Soo Line used to run. Now, it was just a bunch of rusting rails with tall brown grass growing between them.

"I can't believe kids can live way out here and still go to Bainer Junior High," Minna said.

"Where else could they go?" Laura pointed out. "Elk Creek is the only town between here and Cloquet, and that's another fifty miles."

Mrs. Kristiansen turned onto a dirt driveway, where the neat black mailbox read PRINCE.

"I didn't know Dusty lived on a farm," Alice said,

seeing that the ranch-style house was next to a white-boarded barn.

"I don't think it's a farm — I think it's a stable," observed Laura.

Sure enough, two horses stuck their heads out of the white building and looked over at the car. One of them neighed.

"Oh, I love horses!" said Minna, who'd never gotten over reading *Black Beauty* in third grade. "Dusty is so lucky!"

Dusty and Julie came out of the house. *At least Julie isn't smoking,* Alice thought.

"Hi, guys," said Dusty, as she climbed into the front. "Hi, Mrs. Kristiansen."

"Hi, Janet," said Mrs. Kristiansen.

"Hi, Dusty," said the rest of the girls.

"You remember Julie, right?" she said, looking back at them. "Mrs. Kristiansen, this is my friend Julie."

"Hi, Mrs. Kristiansen," said Julie. "It was nice of you to drive all the way out here to pick us up."

"Oh, it's no problem," said Mrs. Kristiansen.

At the mall, the girls didn't have any set plan, except to hang out. Dusty said she needed to get some WD-40 at Kmart for her father.

"Do you own all those horses?" asked Minna, as they started to walk.

"Some of them," said Dusty. 'We take boarders, too."

"You're so lucky," Minna said. "You must get to ride all the time."

"Horses are a lot of work," Dusty said. "But if you'd like to, come over sometime."

"Really?"

Alice thought she saw actual stars in Minna's eyes.

"Sure, any of you guys," she said generously. "Julie and I go riding all the time, don't we, Jules?"

"Yup," said Julie, looking at her friend. "It's a blast."

Dusty slipped into the Kmart and returned with the WD-40.

"Now what should we do?" said Minna.

"Let's go see what's new at the Disc-o-Mat," suggested Laura.

The girls turned and walked toward the end of the mall. As they passed Jo-Ann Fabrics, Alice spotted Yoon Jun Lee and his mother. Mrs. Lee was stooping over to examine a bolt of fabric and Yoon Jun was holding on to her elbow.

Alice hoped that no one else saw them, and she tried to hurry past. But just when she thought she was clear, Mrs. Lee lifted her head and recognized her.

"Hello, Alice," she said, smiling. Yoon Jun looked up at her, but when he saw her looking, he ducked his head down again, like an ostrich.

"Oh, hi," Alice said, as if she had just noticed them.

"How are your parents?" Mrs. Lee asked. "Please tell them thank you again for the beautiful meal!"

"Oh sure," Alice said, shifting from foot to foot. She hoped her friends wouldn't notice she was missing and turn back.

"It's a nice day to be at the mall," Alice said while glancing around. "Geez, but I really have to go. My friends are waiting for me."

"Say hello to your parents," Mrs. Lee said cheerfully.

"Okay, 'bye," Alice said. " 'Bye, Yoon Jun."

"Good-bye," he said.

Chapter 15

❀ ❀ ❀

The last stop of the day was at Orange Julius, where each girl got something to drink. Alice got an extra-large serving because she was thirsty. She looked around warily as she was drinking it, but luckily, there was no sign of the Korean family.

Mrs. Larsen picked them up promptly at three.

"Who gets dropped off first?" she asked.

"Julie," Dusty said. "She lives up County Road W, which joins into the one by my house."

"I can just walk from your house," Julie said.

"We're going to pass by anyway," Dusty said. "Why should you walk that extra way?"

"It's too much trouble," Julie said. "The road is so bad."

"That's no problem," Mrs. Larsen said. "This Wagoneer can go through anything."

"Well, thank you, then," Julie said. "County Road W is the one that runs past the old Bainer Taconite plant."

Julie wasn't kidding about the road. It was full of

holes and so dry that it sent up clouds of dust; within minutes, it looked as if a herd of buffalo had just passed through.

"My," said Mrs. Larsen. "This could be dangerous at night."

What Alice was thinking about was how all the jouncing around was jolting her bladder. She was suddenly feeling the effects of the extra-large Orange Julius.

They twisted around, up a hill, then down.

"It's this one, on the right," Julie said, almost shyly.

The mailbox was stuck in a rusty oil drum. GRAY-WOLF was painted in white letters on the drum.

The house was the most ramshackle building Alice had ever seen: wood, with a sloped roof and small, dark windows. The whole thing seemed to lean unsteadily to one side, as if it was tired and about to lie down.

Alice's bladder suddenly interrupted all her thoughts; alarm bells were clanging in her head.

"Uh, Julie?" she said. Her voice was strained. "Can I use your bathroom?"

Julie seemed to hesitate a second. "Of course," she said. "Follow me."

Alice followed her through a screen door that closed with a loud bang. The house was dark inside, and Alice could hardly see the person watching TV almost in front of her. From the backyard came happy screams of children.

51

"Ma," said Julie, "this is Alice. I said she could use the bathroom."

The person in the overstuffed chair was an enormous woman with short black hair permed around her head like a cap. She looked up at Alice, and Alice saw Julie's same dark eyes and dull skin.

"Hello, Alice," she said, and nodded slightly.

"How do you do?" Alice said. "I'm sorry, I really need to go."

The woman smiled. She had gaps in her teeth. Alice picked her way among a plastic Bigwheel trike racer, a G.I. Joe, and a Tonka dump truck.

"My little brother is always leaving his toys hanging around," Julie said apologetically. "The bathroom is right over there."

Alice shut the door and almost sighed with relief. The bathroom was small, but neat, with rows of crisp towels. The mirror above the sink was spotless.

She finished, washed her hands, and dried them on one of the towels. Then, impulsively, she peeked into the cabinet under the sink, curious to see what kind of bathroom supplies the Graywolfs bought.

There was a pack of generic toilet paper, a bottle of rose milk hand lotion, a bottle of Woolworth's glass cleaner, and some Drano. Alice quietly shut the door. She heard Julie's mom yell something to Julie about needing to get to work.

Alice came out of the bathroom.

"Thanks so much," she said to Julie, who was in

the kitchen, getting out a box of some kind of mix.

"No problem," she said. She started to pour the mix into a large enamel bowl. "It was fun to go to the mall."

"Yeah," said Alice. "See you in school."

Mrs. Larsen then drove Dusty home, and she obliged everyone by waiting so they could have a chance to pet Dusty's horse, Star.

"Isn't Dusty the greatest?" cooed Minna, as they pulled out of the driveway. Star was still sticking his head over the paddock fence.

"She sure is," Alice agreed.

After Minna and Laura were dropped off, Mrs. Larsen turned the car toward home. She had a solemn look on her face. "It's too bad that your friend Julie lives in such poor circumstances," she said.

Alice thought about the sad, dark house and the package of generic toilet paper. "It is," she agreed.

"It's just such a shame that Native Americans so often find themselves in difficult situations."

"Mom, our teacher at school also says 'Native Americans' for Indians," Alice said, suddenly thoughtful. "What's the difference?"

"American Indians aren't really Indians at all," Mrs. Larsen said. "When Columbus landed in North America, he actually thought he was in India, so he naturally called the Native Americans 'Indians.' "

"How lost can you get?" Alice giggled. "America is nowhere *near* India!"

"That's right," Mrs. Larsen said, nodding. "So as a matter of pride, some people think it's better to refer to native American peoples as just that, Native Americans."

"Hm, I wonder if Julie minds, either way," Alice said. She was thinking that there was nothing in their house to suggest that they were Indian — Native American — except that they themselves looked it. It was sort of the same situation with her: she might look Korean, but she would never be caught running around in a kimono or whatever.

Alice now felt a little less harsh toward Julie Graywolf. At first Julie had seemed so tough and awful, smoking those cigarettes, not seeming to care about her appearance. But after seeing even that little slice of her life today, Alice could see more of what Julie was all about, how hard it must be to live in a little house so far from town. She probably couldn't very easily do things like cheerleading or the school paper if her folks had to drive for half an hour to pick her up. And she did seem to be so practical and down-to-earth about everything — it looked like she was doing the cooking for the family tonight. Alice could almost see why Dusty liked her so much.

After all, wasn't it the Native Americans who said that you can't judge a person until you've walked a hundred miles in their moccasins?

Chapter 16

❋ ❋ ❋

Alice plunked her lunch down, only to find another crudely penciled heart in the center of the table. This one was rubbed in even darker than the first one, and it said "Alice Larsen -n- Yoon Jun Lee."

Alice was so mad she couldn't speak. She could only jab her finger at it as her two friends' eyes widened with surprise and disgust.

Yoon Jun Lee was there, at his table, still alone. Alice decided it was time to confront him.

She turned to start walking toward his table. "I'm going to give him a piece of my mind," she said.

"Wait," said Laura. "Are you sure he did it? Do they do the same thing in Korea, with the hearts and all that?"

"Maybe they do," Alice said. "Or else he seems to catch on to some things real fast."

"He's probably seen stuff like this all over the bathroom walls," added Minna. "I heard that the

55

boys' bathroom is *covered* with stuff like that — and maybe he's even writing some more in there."

Alice started walking. She was sure he had done it. She could hear Minna and Laura following her.

"Yoon Jun," she said, when she reached his table, "I am not your girlfriend — would you quit writing that?"

Yoon Jun Lee's head raised, then lowered. His mouth trembled a little as he stole nervous glances at the three angry girls. "I — I not understand," he said.

"You know, the stupid hearts." Alice drew an expansive heart in the air with one hand.

"No — not understand," he said, alarmed.

Alice stepped in a little closer. He wouldn't get off by playing dumb. She could smell something garlicky reeking from his lunch. She hated garlic.

"Just cut it out, okay?" she said. "It's not funny."

"No, no," he said, shaking his head. He looked panicked.

He probably wouldn't do it again, now that he knew she was so angry at him, Alice thought with some satisfaction. She turned around, and Laura and Minna wordlessly followed.

Back at the table, they scrubbed the pencil marks off again. When Alice glanced back at the table, Yoon Jun Lee was gone.

"I can see where he thinks you're cute," said Minna. "But the nerve of him."

After lunch, as the three girls were heading to the

56

bathroom they passed Yoon Jun in the hall. He seemed to be talking to Travis Jones. A small crowd of kids had gathered around them.

"What's this?" said Laura curiously. Alice could tell she was sniffing out another story.

"Let's see you karate chop, huh?" said Travis, holding out his arm. "Karate chop my arm, Chinaman. Don't all Chinese know karate?"

Yoon Jun looked scared and a little mad. He tried backing away from Travis, but Travis kept following.

"Just one chop, Chinaman," he said. "Gimme one little chop."

Alice felt sick. She hated Travis Jones, and she felt really sorry for Yoon Jun Lee, despite the heart graffiti and everything. He looked so confused. But like everyone else in the crowd, she would never say anything to Travis Jones — what if he decided to start picking on her next, like last year? And also, he was large and always wore ripped T-shirts, so you could see how big his muscles were.

"Leave him alone, Travis — you make me want to puke!" Dusty Prince had broken through the crowd and was shoving everybody away, including Alice, Minna, and Laura.

"You've got some real problems, boy," she said, her teeth clenched. "If you want a karate chop so bad, I'll give you one."

Dusty stood up straight, and she was, indeed, just as tall as Travis. He looked around uneasily.

"You just watch yourself, Prince," he muttered, then he turned around and skulked away, flexing his muscles.

Yoon Jun Lee gave Dusty a grateful smile. It was the first time Alice had ever seen him smile.

"It's okay," Dusty said, patting him on the arm in a way that Alice imagined she'd pat her horse. "He's really just a big baby."

Then she turned around and glared at the kids still hanging around. To their astonishment, her gaze seemed to land on Alice, Minna, and Laura the longest.

"Good for nothing," she said, and turned and walked down the hall.

"What'd *we* do?" said Minna nervously.

"I think," said Laura, "it was what we didn't do."

Chapter 17

❀ ❀ ❀

"How is our friend, Yoon Jun Lee, coming along in school?" asked Reverend Larsen that night at dinner.

Alice chewed her mouthful of peas, then swallowed. Yoon Jun Lee was the last thing she wanted to discuss.

"I don't know, Daddy." She crossed her fingers under the table. *White lie,* she said to herself. "We don't hang around in the same groups."

Her father stroked his bearded chin. Alice always thought that he looked like "Pa" from *Little House in the Big Woods* when he did that.

"Yoon Jun is very smart, you know. His mother tells me that he won a very important history prize back in Korea."

Alice tried not to fidget. She didn't see what this had to do with *her.*

"But I guess he hasn't been doing all that well in school here — Mrs. Lee thinks he might be lonely," Reverend Larsen said slowly. "Of course, it would be hard for anyone to adjust to a new school, even more if you're coming from a different country and aren't entirely comfortable with the language."

Alice held her breath. She hoped he wasn't getting at what she thought he was getting at.

"So don't you think that the right and Christian thing to do would be to help out where we can?"

Alice let her breath out. She looked at her mother, who excused herself to get more Tater Tots.

"Like what?"

"Since you happen to be in his class, there are a bunch of things you can do — talk to him in the halls, eat lunch with him, maybe even take him out to a movie with your friends once in a while."

Alice couldn't believe her ears. "Daddy, do you know that he writes things like 'Yoon Jun Lee loves Alice Larsen' on the cafeteria tables — *in large letters?*"

Ha, she thought, *that ought to get him.*

To Alice's surprise, he chuckled. "Okay, so he's got good taste. Now listen — "

"Da–dee!" Alice wailed. "You don't understand."

"Jack," said Mrs. Larsen warningly. Reverend Larsen frowned slightly at his wife.

"Alice," he said calmly, "it's never as bad as you think. God never gives a person more than he or she can bear."

"You're not God," Alice said miserably.

"No, you're right. But my responsibility is to do

God's work on earth. Now, you remember the Golden Rule, don't you?"

Alice shifted in her seat. Of course she knew the Golden Rule. "Do unto others as you would have others do unto you."

"Precisely. Now, pretend that you're someone who's lived in Korea all your life, and you suddenly find yourself plopped down in Bainer.

"So you're with all these kids you don't know, but who know each other," he went on. "And maybe you don't speak the language so well, so you end up being alone a lot.

"Then say someone comes out of the blue to be friends with you, show you around and things — wouldn't you be happy that person did that?"

"I guess," Alice said. She did feel sorry for Yoon Jun, especially knowing that he spent his Saturdays at the mall with his mother. He must be lonely with no one but Travis Jones paying any attention to him.

"Now, if I were in junior high, I could go and be friends with this boy Yoon Jun and do my good works. But I'm not, and since you are, I guess I'd like to put the burden on you — and I realize it is a burden when you have your own friends and activities — but I would be very proud of you if you would help make this boy's adjustment to Bainer Junior High just a little bit easier."

Alice was silent. It all sounded so good, so noble, like it ought to be a pleasure to do. And she loved doing "good works" for her father. But this was nothing like visiting old people in the nursing home. When she thought about talking to Yoon Jun in school — much less eating lunch with him — it made her toes curl. What would Minna and Laura say?

"You're an even better emissary of good will," her father went on. "You're already someone Yoon Jun can feel comfortable with, someone who already looks familiar to him and who fits in beautifully, too."

Now, this was going way too far, Alice thought. No one should link her with Yoon Jun Lee just because an accident of nature made them look somewhat similar. That wasn't fair!

"Does this have something to do with my slanty Chinaman eyes?" She hated to say something Travis Jones would probably say, but in a way her father *was* acting like Travis Jones.

"Alice!" said Mrs. Larsen. She looked as if she was going to cry.

"You have *pretty* eyes," Mary said gravely.

"Please don't talk about yourself that way," said Reverend Larsen. "That's not what I meant."

"Then what did you mean?"

Alice's father didn't answer her. He just put his head down and brooded. Alice became scared; usually her father could never be shaken out of his even, cheerful mood. But she didn't regret one word that she'd said, not one. If someone wanted to link her up with Yoon Jun Lee, they'd better find a better reason than something about them having the same skin or eyes — that had nothing to do with the kind of people they were.

Alice left the table, glad it was Mary's night to dry the dishes. She went up to her room and shut the door, but not quite all the way.

Later, she heard her parents arguing from the kitchen.

"I wish you would just ease up on poor Alice . . ." Her mother's voice.

". . . the poor girl's going to have an identity crisis."

"Look, Yoon Jun Lee could use a little human kindness. It won't kill Alice. You saw how shy he is."

Huh, Alice thought. *Shy enough to write stupid things on cafeteria tables.*

"Karen," said her father. Then it got all muffled. Alice wondered if her parents suddenly realized she was listening. Since they were in the kitchen, she couldn't use her glass-against-the-wall trick.

She hated Yoon Jun Lee. She wished he'd never come to Bainer. Before he came to town, her life had been going so well.

* * *

"Hey, you sound depressed," said Troy when he called her that night. He'd been calling her once a week for the last two weeks — at least something in her life was going right.

"Oh, it's just been a long day," Alice said. She longed to talk about her problem with him, but she didn't want Troy to know that she had anything to do with that Yoon Jun Lee. Sometimes she even felt funny talking to Minna or Laura about it.

"You going to the dance next week?" he asked.

"Oh sure, are you?"

"I guess," said Troy. "Coach is even letting us out of practice for it, since it's right after school."

"Are Pete and Dean going?" Alice asked. She heard Troy laugh. She liked his laugh, it was a low, gravelly chuckle.

"You a little matchmaker or something?"

"Oh no," Alice said innocently. "I'm just wondering."

"Tell Minna and Laura that they'll be there," he said good-naturedly. "And don't *you* forget to go."

"I won't," Alice said. Suddenly, she felt so much better.

Chapter 18

❀ ❀ ❀

The Bainer Junior High cafeteria didn't look like the Bainer Junior High cafeteria. There were orange and black crepe paper streamers and plastic Halloween pumpkins hanging from the ceiling, and the long rows of tables and benches had been folded up and neatly wheeled over to the side wall. Alice glanced over at the spot by the door, almost expecting Yoon Jun Lee to be there, but of course he wasn't. She doubted that a dance would be his kind of thing.

Alice, Minna, and Laura were standing on one side of the room with the rest of the girls, including Dusty Prince and the other eighth-grade cheerleaders. The boys stood on the other side. They were guffawing and pushing each other and generally trying to act as though there wasn't a dance going on.

Alice turned to Dusty and asked, "Where's Julie?"

Dusty took a few seconds to stare at her, without smiling. Lately, she had been doing that every time Alice or Minna or Laura talked to her. It was almost as though she didn't want to talk to them if she could help it.

"She's home," Dusty said, finally. Then she added, "Julie does more work than anybody I know. She has a babysitting job but also has to take care of her little brother and sister because her mother works weird hours."

"Wow," said Alice. She always assumed she was too young to be thinking about real work. Her parents gave her an allowance that paid for everything, so she couldn't conceive of having a real job like Julie or Yoon Jun Lee. Maybe when she was in high school, she'd get a job at Woolworth's or Dairy Queen so she could have more money for clothes, but high school was very far off.

"This kid I know, Yoon Jun Lee, has a real job, too," Alice said.

"Hmf," said Dusty suddenly, and she turned and walked away.

Alice felt a quick fear stabbing at her. Could it be that Dusty was *still* mad from that time Travis Jones was teasing Yoon Jun? And if so, did that mean she was going to be mad forever? That would be worse than having her kicked off cheerleading.

"Hey," said Minna, nudging her in the side and suddenly breaking up all her thoughts, "maybe if they'd play some Sid the Killer, people would want to dance."

"The boys look awful shy," Laura said dubiously.

66

They did play a Sid the Killer song; in fact, it was Minna's favorite, "The Flies of Summer." Alice and Laura watched with admiration as she marched across the floor and asked Dean Jacobs to dance. Of course he said yes. Alice also noticed that Chet Armstrong, the captain of the football team, was dancing with Dusty.

Finally enough kids were dancing that the boys started to get more into it. Troy asked Alice to dance, and Pete asked Laura. Almost the second they were on the dance floor, the song changed to a slow one.

Alice shut her eyes as she swayed to the music with Troy. She liked being close to him. When she opened her eyes next, she saw a kid waving a cardboard heart at them. There were a few other kids doing the same thing to some other couples.

"What's this?" Alice whispered to Troy.

"We're supposed to kiss when they do that," said Troy. While Alice was thinking about this, he kissed her, right on the mouth!

"Oh!" said Alice.

"Is that okay?" said Troy. He was grinning madly.

"Of course." Alice's face was on fire. "Can we do it again?"

Troy gave her a long kiss this time. Alice heard Dean yell, "Hey Troyster! Come up for air already!"

When Alice opened her eyes, she found Yoon Jun Lee staring right at her. He was in a crowd of kids watching the dancers.

"Our friend from Country Kitchen," said Troy, when he saw her looking at Yoon Jun.

"Oh yeah," said Alice quickly. "He's weird, isn't he?"

"I don't know," said Troy. "I've never talked to him."

Alice couldn't figure out why Yoon Jun Lee was at the dance if all he was going to do was stare at people and make them uncomfortable.

Why should I feel uncomfortable? she thought suddenly. *For once in my life I want to have a good time and not worry about Yoon Jun Lee.*

The song changed to a fast one, and Alice turned her back on Yoon Jun Lee and danced like a maniac.

Chapter 19

✿ ✿ ✿

At the end of the dance, Alice and Troy found Minna and Dean, and Laura and Pete. All of them were sweaty but happy-looking. They milled around just outside the cafeteria door as some parents started wandering in, looking for their kids.

Alice saw a man in a red hunting cap staring at her. His face was covered with stubble, and his eyes were red around the rims.

"You're the second one I seen!" he said, pointing his finger at her. "You slanty-eyed gooks are taking over this goddamn town!"

Alice's mouth opened, then shut. She had no idea what "gooks" were, but she knew it wasn't good.

"Hey — you'd better apologize to Alice right now!" yelled Troy. His voice cracked a little.

The man in the hunting cap glared at him. "Shut up, ya little gook-lover," the man snarled. He fished through the crowd until he found Travis Jones.

"C'mon!" he yelled at Travis, grabbing him by the

scruff of his neck. "What're you doing wasting time at some dance that's full of gooks!"

"We should tell someone," said Troy. Alice was surprised to see tears in his eyes.

Then, as if it were planned, Alice's father walked in.

"Reverend Larsen!" Minna yelped. "There was this guy in here calling Alice a 'gook,' or something like that."

The smile disappeared from Alice's father's face, and she heard him suck in his breath sharply.

"Who said this?" he asked Alice.

"I think the guy was the dad of this kid in my class, Travis Jones," Alice said miserably.

"Jones," said Reverend Larsen, stroking his beard. Alice noticed that his hand was shaking a little.

"What should we do?" asked Troy. His fists were clenched.

Reverend Larsen bowed his head, as he did when he led the congregation in prayer.

"Kids," he said, looking at all of them. "What Mr. Jones said was very bad, but I don't think he's actually a bad man. He was in a terrible war, and he's very troubled. I don't think he knows what he's saying."

"But look at what he's doing to his kids, then!" Laura protested. "Remember, last year, Travis Jones teased Alice until the teacher made him stop."

"And he's been teasing that new kid, Yoon Jun Lee," added Minna.

Reverend Larsen looked worried. Alice wanted him

70

to be angry. How could he let someone — an adult especially — say something so bad to her!

"Uh, Reverend Larsen, what does 'gook' mean, anyway?" asked Laura.

Reverend Larsen flinched. "It's just a bad word, Laura," he said.

"I've got a few bad words of my own for Mr. Jones," said Alice resolutely. She tried to think of every bad word she had ever heard of.

"Just forget about it, Alice, and the rest of you," said Reverend Larsen. "I know it's hard to understand, but there are some people in this world who are so angry at themselves that they take it out on others, when they don't mean to."

"How can I just forget it?" said Alice. She wanted to scream, and she felt tears rising in her eyes. "He sure sounded like he meant it — and I think he is a mean, mean person!"

Reverend Larsen took Alice in his big arms. "Please, honey," he said, "just do it for me, okay?"

Alice could hear an awful pain in her father's voice. If she didn't leave soon, she'd just start bawling. "Let's go, Dad," she gulped.

At home, Alice said she wanted to be alone. For the first time in a long while, she let herself think about her parents — the Korean ones — way on the other side of the world. Had they ever loved her? Did they know when they gave her up that she would grow up in a place where people could call her names?

Travis Jones's dad had probably seen Yoon Jun first, then her. But he called them the same name, like they were the same person. Why? She was not a bit like Yoon Jun Lee. Did Travis Jones's father know that she was a cheerleader? That she didn't have an accent? That she hardly knew that a place called Korea existed?

Why couldn't she have blond curls like her sister? She would give anything to fit in and leave everything about Korea behind.

Chapter 20

❀ ❀ ❀

Alice had to see Travis Jones in homeroom that following Wednesday. She was half hoping he'd apologize for his father, but he didn't. He was up to his usual tricks, talking loudly and pushing people's books off their desks.

Mrs. Choquette was telling them about International Day, which was to be held the third week of November.

"As you know," she said. "Bainer Junior High holds an International Day, where students, in teams of two, bring food that represents their heritage, and everyone presents a report on that country. You can even wear costumes if you'd like to be more authentic."

"What if we're a bunch of stuff?" asked Fred Jorich. "Like I'm part German, Welsh, Polish, and one-sixteenth Chippewa Indian."

"You can just pick out one country from your or

your partner's background," she said. "Especially if you have something in common."

"Don't do Germany — sauerkraut smells like barf!" called Travis Jones, from the back of the room.

"He should talk," Minna whispered to Alice. "He's the one with Swamp Thing for a father."

"Mr. Jones," Mrs. Choquette said evenly, "please raise your hand if you have something to add to the discussion."

At least they were going to do this with partners, Alice thought. Her mom and dad were one hundred percent Norwegian, so she could do it with Laura, and they could bring in Norwegian goodies like *lefse* and *lutefisk*. Maybe all three of them could be together; after all, Minna's mom was part Norwegian. Maybe they could all dress up in silly costumes or something fun like that.

"We're going to do this by homeroom," Mrs. Choquette said. "Now, in this hat I have two sets of numbers one through thirteen to cover the twenty-six of you. Everyone picks a number, and the person who has your number will be your partner."

Alice and Minna immediately exchanged worried looks. They were thinking about what would happen if they got someone like Travis Jones — or Yoon Jun Lee. What a dumb idea to force partners on people.

"If we already know someone we have something in common with," Alice glanced meaningfully over at

Minna, "can't we just have them as partners?"

Mrs. Choquette smiled patiently, as if she'd just explained all this. "If we did that, Alice," she said, "we'd probably get a lot of similar projects. If you have a randomly assigned partner, there are all sorts of unexpected things you can dig up about each others's backgrounds."

That was exactly what she did not want to do, Alice thought.

Please, please, please let me get Minna! she prayed. *No one can say anything bad about being Norwegian.*

The hat was passed, and when it came to Alice, she held her breath for good luck. All the slips of paper looked the same. She tried to pick one near the spot where Minna had taken hers, hoping that maybe Mrs. Choquette hadn't shuffled the numbers well once she threw them into the hat.

She drew number twelve, which was better than number thirteen, she supposed.

"I have seven, what do you have?" asked Minna.

Alice's heart sank. "Twelve," she whispered back.

Mrs. Choquette then had everyone call out their numbers one by one, and people with the same numbers had to go stand by their partners.

Travis Jones had gotten number thirteen. Alice sighed with relief.

"Seven," said Minna.

"That's me," said Fred Jorich, Mr. One-sixteenth Chippewa.

Alice chewed on an imaginary hangnail. "Twelve," she said.

No one said anything. Alice looked around.

"Number twelve," said Mrs. Choquette. "Who's got number twelve?"

"Oh, I num-bah twelve," said Yoon Jun Lee. His face lit up, as though he thought Alice had picked him on purpose.

Travis Jones snickered. "First comes love, then comes marriage . . ."

"Be quiet, Mr. Jones," Mrs. Choquette said to him. "Yoon Jun, go over and stand by Alice."

Yoon Jun obediently got up and shuffled over to Alice and Minna's side of the room. When he got there, he looked at the floor. Alice couldn't believe this was happening.

"Now," Mrs. Choquette said, when they were all done, "you might think three weeks is a long time, but it's not. Remember, your parents will be there to hear the reports, so make sure you do a nice job, and don't put everything off until the last minute."

The bell rang. When Alice happened to glance Yoon Jun's way, he sort of smiled, before ducking his head again.

Chapter 21

❀ ❀ ❀

The phone rang during dinner. Mrs. Larsen was in the kitchen getting out more baked potatoes, so she picked it up.

"Alice, it's for you," she said. Alice ran to the kitchen and picked up the phone that her mother had left lying on the counter.

"Hello?"

"Hello, Al-ice?" questioned the voice, and Alice knew immediately who it was by the accent. "This is Yoon Jun Lee, from school?"

"Hi," she said. "I bet you called about the project."

"The school project?" he said, or asked — she couldn't tell which. "You want to do something on Korea? My mother says she cook."

"I haven't really thought about the project," Alice said, a little crossly. She kept thinking of the stupid things he had written on the cafeteria tables, and the stupid things Travis Jones's father had said. She wished she could stay as far away from Yoon Jun Lee as possible.

"My mom can just as easily make *lefse,* which is a Norwegian food."

At the mention of *"lefse,"* Mrs. Larsen's head bobbed up. Alice waved to her to let her know she'd be off the phone soon.

"We can talk about it later — we're in the middle of eating dinner," Alice said. "I really don't care either way."

"Okay?" he said happily. "We talk in school tomorrow?"

"Okay, 'bye," said Alice, dropping the phone as if it were contaminated. She had no idea how she was going to get through the next three weeks.

"For International Day," she announced to her family, "I got that kid, Yoon Jun Lee, as my partner in a lottery. We're fighting over whether to do Korean or Norwegian for our food project. Minna told me that Laura, the lucky, got to be partners with Dina Petrilli. You know, her father owns Petrilli's Pasta Place, the one with the really yummy raviolis."

"Yum," said Mary. "I wish I were going to be there."

"International Day is a great idea," said Reverend Larsen, just as Alice knew he would. "It's a great way to learn about other cultures."

*   *   *

The next day, Yoon Jun Lee approached Alice in the lunch room. The pudginess of his face made him look sort of like a sad turtle.

"We can do Korean, yes?" he said, smiling slightly. Alice was sure she was going to expire, right in front of her friends.

"Your partner?" said Laura, cocking an eyebrow at her. Alice hadn't broken the bad news yet.

"Yes," said Alice. "Yes, let's do Korean — anything you say."

She hoped he'd leave, pronto, and he did. He shuffled back to his usual table and unpacked his lunch. Alice noticed that Fred Jorich and a couple of other kids had joined him at the table by the door.

"Well, now at least you'll learn about Korea like your parents always wanted you to," Minna said philosophically.

"Only my dad is into that," said Alice. "My mom feels pretty much the same way I do. Anyway, I only said we'd do it because I'd rather not waste time arguing with him."

"I wonder if he's still in love with you," said Laura.

Alice made a face at her.

Chapter 22

❀ ❀ ❀

Besides all the International Day hassles, Alice was worried because Minna had also begun to think that Dusty was giving them the cold shoulder in cheerleading. She wasn't mean or anything, she just didn't hang around with them the way she used to, and she always stared at them without smiling whenever either of them spoke to her.

"Maybe we should talk to her," said Minna, when they were on the way to lunch. "And find out what's wrong."

"I guess," Alice said. She had the nagging feeling that it had something to do with the time Travis Jones was teasing Yoon Jun Lee. All Yoon Jun did was make her life miserable.

Alice and Minna waited until practice was over to talk to Dusty.

"Dusty?" said Alice timidly, as practice was breaking up.

"Yeah?" said Dusty. Alice cringed. She felt like a

wobbly house of cards that Dusty could blow down any minute.

"Uh, Dusty," said Alice. "Minna and I were just wondering something."

Dusty was staring at them levelly.

Alice couldn't go on — Dusty was too wonderful. They must really be scumbags if she was shunning them.

"Are you mad at us?" finished Minna. Alice could see that she was scared, too.

"Why should I be mad at you?" said Dusty, but she didn't sound very happy, either.

"I don't know," said Minna, and then she bit her lip and looked at Alice.

Alice decided to speak up and be brave — Dusty would hopefully be impressed by that.

"It seems like maybe you've stopped talking with us ever since the time you stopped Travis Jones from teasing that Yoon Jun Lee kid in the hall."

Dusty crossed her arms and smiled wryly. "It seems like maybe I don't enjoy hanging around with people who don't stand up for their own friends," she said simply, but she had a look on her face that said she thought she had just said something very, very profound.

"What do you mean?" said Alice.

The arms came uncrossed. "Oh come *on*," she said impatiently. She looked right at Alice. "I see you talking to that Japanese kid sometimes at lunch or what-

81

ever, and the next time I see him, Travis Jones is teasing him, and there you are, looking on with the rest of the kids like the whole thing was set up for your amusement."

"Alice isn't really friends with Yoon Jun Lee," said Minna. "His family has met her family through church."

"So what's the big deal?" Dusty barked. "You *know* him, don't you? I wouldn't stand for Travis Jones ragging on my worst enemy — and here you two let him hassle someone you *know!*"

Then, as if Dusty was afraid she might explode if she stayed around any longer, she turned and ran down the junior high lawn, her long legs lengthening into an impressive canter. Alice wondered where she was going.

"Maybe she would've thought differently if she'd known about the things Yoon Jun Lee was writing on the tables," Minna suggested helpfully.

Alice felt hopeless. Things were worse than when they started. And, once again, it all boiled down to one Yoon Jun Lee. If he hadn't come to their school, Travis Jones wouldn't have teased him, and Dusty Prince wouldn't be mad at them right now.

Chapter 23

❀ ❀ ❀

Even though Alice would have liked to put off the International Day project until the next century, she realized that she and Yoon Jun Lee had better get working on it; Minna wasn't exactly thrilled about doing hers with Fred Jorich, either, but they'd already compiled a whole stack of notes for their report.

At lunch, Alice marched over to where Yoon Jun was sitting — his usual spot — and told him she'd meet him after school in the library and that he should remember to bring a notebook and pens. She didn't even wait for him to reply but instead turned on her heel and rejoined Minna and Laura.

After school, Alice went straight to the Bainer Public Library. Yoon Jun Lee was already there, sitting at a table near the bust of Noah Webster. Piled up on a chair next to him were his jacket and a bunch of schoolbooks: bio, math, science, and English.

Gads, she thought. *Does he take all his books home every night — and does he study them?*

He smiled a little when he saw her. He seemed not to realize that if it weren't for this project, she would have no reason to talk to him for the rest of their time at the Bainer public school system.

"Let's get to work," Alice said. She lugged over the J–K volume of the *World Book Encyclopedia.*

"Korea has a very interesting history," Yoon Jun started (saying it like "intahlesting histolee"). "It has been invaded by lots of different countries. Now, it is two parts of one."

"Uh-huh," said Alice, opening the *World Book.* In looking up "Korea," she passed some diagrams on how to knit, under "Knitting." They looked interesting, but she resisted the temptation to even pause. She wanted to get this project done as quickly as possible.

There were about ten whole pages on Korea, plus maps. Alice groaned to herself. Now, how was she going to find out what was important in all this *stuff?*

"Korea," she read, "is a land in Eastern Asia that consists of two nations. One is the Republic of Korea — usually called *South Korea.* Seoul is the capital . . ."

How boring! she thought. She skipped to the "Facts in Brief." Under South Korea, she read:

"Capital: Seoul.

Official Language: Korean.

Official Name: *Taehan-minguk* (Republic of Korea)."

"*Taehan-minguk?*" she muttered. What kind of gibberish was that?

"*Taehan-minguk?*" repeated Yoon Jun Lee. "That is South Korea. You speak good Korean."

"I wasn't speaking it," Alice said. "I was reading it from the encyclopedia."

"It sound good to me," said Yoon Jun, and he smiled again.

Alice noticed that he had a thick book, *The History of the Korean Peninsula,* open in front of him. It looked like something difficult from the adult section — something she'd never try.

"Is that a good book?" she asked.

"Very good. Many interesting facts on why the Koreans, who are one people, have never really had one country to themselves."

"You aren't copying word for word, are you?" she asked, a little suspiciously. "We're not supposed to do that on reports."

"Oh no," said Yoon Jun, very piously. "I read. Then I write about what I have read."

Alice was a little skeptical. If he could read so well, why couldn't he talk better?

Yoon Jun kept his nose in the book for over an hour, seemingly never getting tired or bored. Alice had gotten up twice to go to the bathroom, once to look at the Readers' Week exhibit, and once to check out some Judy Blume books.

She had been listlessly writing a lot of stuff about rice and Buddhism, but she'd found very little to spark her interest, except the descriptions of Koreans' looks:

"The Koreans resemble the Chinese and the Japanese. Most Koreans have broad faces, straight black hair, olive-brown skin, and dark eyes that appear to be slanted because of an inner eyelid fold."

The way they described Koreans sounded gross! Broad faces . . . olive-brown skin (mud-colored?) . . . inner eyelid fold, and slanted eyes? She hated the dumb *World Book*. It also made it sound as though she and Yoon Jun Lee and all the Chinese and Japanese people looked exactly alike — which was ridiculous. How could she trust anything else it had to say about Korea or the Koreans?

Alice looked over at Yoon Jun, who was still bent over his book. He paused to write something in his loose-leaf notebook. His nose was greasy.

"Why don't we make Xeroxes for each other of our notes?" Alice suggested. What she really wanted to do was take a walk to the copy machine.

"Okay," said Yoon Jun, and he surrendered his loose-leaf notebook. He must have had at least ten pages of single-spaced notes. Alice felt a little guilty about having only three pages. She gathered everything up and dug out her change.

"Do you need money?" asked Yoon Jun.

"No, no," Alice said, thinking that paying for the Xerox sort of made up for her lack of notes. Gratefully, she stretched her legs as she walked to the copy machine.

When she got back, Yoon Jun's nose was still buried in his book. He looked so thoughtful that Alice impulsively asked him, "Yoon Jun, do you know what the word *gook* means?"

Yoon Jun looked up at her and frowned. "That very bad word," he said gravely. "American soldiers come up with it in the Korean War as name for Koreans. It come from a word *hanguk,* which mean Korea. But the *guk* part just means country. Like America is *miguk.* Those Americans surprise me sometimes with how stupid they are. With their way, they are 'gooks' too!"

"They don't understand the Korean language very well, then, do they?" said Alice.

"No way," said Yoon Jun. "In fact, remember when I see you at the dance? This guy there, he call me 'gook' afterward 'cause he think I *Vietnamese!* Now that is dumb. Koreans don't look like Vietnamese at all."

"Of course he shouldn't have said *anything,*" said Alice.

"That is true," said Yoon Jun. "But before we come to America, friends warn us that there are people who no like Asians. Even some American GIs in Seoul no like Koreans, so I ready. Still, I see that lots of people want to be friends with *you,* and that make me happy."

Alice felt tears unexpectedly forming in her eyes, and she turned her head quickly. *This was pudgy old Yoon Jun Lee, for heaven's sake, the one who writes on cafeteria tables.*

Mrs. Larsen showed up promptly at four-thirty. Alice asked Yoon Jun if he needed a ride, and he said thank you, that would be nice. So Mrs. Larsen drove uptown and dropped him and his tons of books off in front of the Belmor Apartment Complex, which was otherwise known as "The Projects." It looked dark and slightly sinister from the outside. He waved and then was swallowed up by the building.

Chapter 24

❀ ❀ ❀

About a week before International Day, during one of their note-taking sessions, Yoon Jun suddenly asked Alice if she would come over to his house for dinner.

"That way," said Yoon Jun, "you can know what the food is like before the other kids try."

Alice cringed a little. Although the last few times that she'd spent with Yoon Jun weren't as torturous as she'd dreaded, she still had it in her mind that she'd like to spend as little time as possible with him.

"My mother is good cook," he added encouragingly.

On the other hand, she thought, *What if Yoon Jun shows up at International Day with squid's eyes, or lizard eggs — or cat? Maybe it'd be a good idea to see what Korean cooking is all about.*

"Okay, good idea," Alice said. Then she got a little annoyed at seeing how delighted Yoon Jun became;

did he still have that absurd crush on her? she wondered.

"It's important that we have a good all-around presentation," she added formally.

The next day at lunch, Alice informed Minna and Laura. "Guess who I'm having dinner with on Thursday?"

"Troy?" guessed Minna.

"The Pope?" asked Laura.

"No," Alice said. "With Yoon Jun buddy over there." She hooked her thumb in the general direction of the cafeteria door.

"What?" squealed Minna.

"Does this have something to do with International Day?" inquired Laura.

"Precisely," said Alice. "Poison control."

"What are they serving?" asked Minna. "Cat eggrolls?"

"That's what I need to find out," Alice said gravely.

"Where do they live?" asked Minna.

"The Projects."

"Really?" said Minna. "I thought only druggies and high school dropouts lived there — not families."

"I thought so, too," said Alice.

"Have you learned anything about Korea, by the way?" asked Laura.

"Not a whole lot," Alice admitted. "Yoon Jun is doing a lot of the heavy-duty research."

"Wow, how'd you manage that?" said Minna. "Fred is such a slow reader — he still uses his fingers to follow the words — and I end up getting impatient and doing most of the stuff."

"Yoon Jun is actually a really good reader," Alice said. "He reads books from the adult section. But since he doesn't speak so well, I'm going to do the presentation."

"That's a pretty good deal," said Laura. She looked thoughtfully at her lunch. "Does he ever use any of his personal experiences in the research?"

"Not that I know of," said Alice. "In fact, I don't even know what happened to his dad, like if he's back in Korea, or dead, or what."

Alice paused. She hadn't realized before now that she even cared — that she kind of wanted to know.

"It's interesting," continued Laura, "because even the Petrillis, who I thought were so Italian, have been living in Bainer forever — even the old grandparents were born here."

"Then what's this 'secret family recipe' and 'authentic Italian flavor' business?" said Minna suspiciously.

"The recipes, I supposed, are from Italy," said Laura. "But the rest is all false advertising. Even Mr. Petrilli barely speaks Italian, except for all the 'mama mias' he does whenever you're in the store."

"I've been 'mama mia'ed plenty of times," Minna

said indignantly. "Maybe I'll just eat Jeno's Pizza Rolls — that's probably more authentic."

"Probably," said Laura. "But Alice, you'll be getting the real stuff."

"If it's not too gross," said Alice. "You guys can try it on International Day."

"Oh yeah," said Minna.

Chapter 25

❀ ❀ ❀

At six o'clock sharp, Reverend Larsen drove Alice over to the Belmor Apartments.

"You have fun," he said cheerfully to his daughter.

"*You* have fun," Alice said, a little less cheerfully. Tonight her mother had made macaroni and cheese, one of her favorites. Figures.

Alice walked in the door of the building. Next to it, a sign read SPECIAL MONTHLY RATES. She could hear some harsh strains of heavy metal bleeding out into the dark hallways.

Alice threaded her way down the hall, which was filled with junk: a baby carriage, bikes, a lawn mower. The only light came from a few badly spaced bulbs.

She squinted at the numbers on the doors until she came to 12C. In front of the door was a green plastic welcome mat that said SMILE BECAUSE GOD LOVES YOU. There was no noise coming from inside, but light glowed from behind the frosted glass. She knocked.

Yoon Jun answered the door in his stocking feet. "Hello, Al-ice," he said, opening the door wide.

Alice stepped into a tiny apartment. The living room was about the size of her room at home, and in it was stuffed a sofa, a chair, and a TV set. It was all very neat, but the room was so small she couldn't escape the feeling of claustrophobia.

"Should I take off my shoes?" Alice asked, noting the neat line of sneakers and ladies' sensible shoes at the door.

"You no need to," said Yoon Jun. "My mother just want to try to keep house clean."

"That makes sense," said Alice. She kicked off her shoes and added them to the line. She tried to imagine her father, formal in his collar, running around the house in his black socks, which usually had holes in them. She stifled a giggle.

"We say hi to my mother?" said Yoon Jun. It was then that Alice noticed there wasn't much in the way of cooking smells in the tiny apartment, except for a sharp, slightly pungent vegetable odor. Maybe Korean food wasn't cooked?

Yoon Jun led her behind a wall to an impossibly cramped kitchen; it was so small that Mrs. Lee looked like a giant among all the clutter.

"So nice to see you again, Alice." She smiled, taking Alice's hands in both of hers. "How are parents?"

"They're fine," she said, glancing at the narrow

counters. They were filled with bowls and bowls of fresh vegetables, pickled things, soy sauce, and what looked like raw beef.

"They say hi and sent you this." Alice produced a box of Whitman's Samplers, the kind the Larsens always brought when they ate at someone's house.

"Thank you very much," said Mrs. Lee, saying it like "velly much." "Now, Yoon Jun will set up the table, and I explain to you what everything is."

Yoon Jun got a folding table out of the closet and plunked it in the middle of the living room. Then he got out three chairs and carefully placed them around the table. He then went back to the closet and dug out what looked to Alice like an electric griddle, the kind her mother made pancakes on for Sunday brunch.

Alice jokingly asked him, "Going to make pancakes?"

Yoon Jun looked puzzled. Alice wished she hadn't tried to make a joke. How would he know what pancakes were?

"Pancakes." Yoon Jun's face suddenly lit up. "That same thing as 'griddle cakes'?"

"Why, yes," said Alice.

"Then we have Korean kind of pancakes tonight," he said delightedly.

"Where did you ever hear of 'griddle cakes'?" asked Alice. "That's such an old-fashioned word."

"I read American books, *Little House in the Big*

Woods and *Little House on the Prairie*," he said proudly.

"You read those books?" Alice said incredulously. "Those were my favorite books when I was a little kid."

"Oh yes," Yoon Jun said. "I have uncle who lives here, and he send me these books to better learn English. And these books about Minnesota, so I can imagine what it like."

Alice couldn't help laughing. "You must have been so disappointed when you actually got here," she said. "No covered wagons, bears, or log houses."

"Oh no," said Yoon Jun. "I very happy to see all this wood, all this space with no houses, no nothing. Seoul is very crowded."

Yoon Jun returned to the kitchen, and brought out the food. All the little bowls just barely fit on the table, along with the griddle. Mrs. Lee put a little sesame oil on it, and then she brought in a bowl of batter.

"This Korean food is easy to make," she said. "Is just green beans and flour. We call it *pin dae duk.*"

With a flourish, she poured the batter onto the griddle exactly as if she were making pancakes. She expertly flipped them.

"We say grace, yes?" said Mrs. Lee, after a pile of the steaming pancakes was on each of their plates. She shut her eyes and bowed her head.

Chapter 26

❀ ❀ ❀

"God is good, God is great, and we thank him for this food. By his hand we all are fed, God give us our daily bread. Amen."

"Amen," said Alice, trying not to laugh. She hadn't heard that grace since she was about six years old. "Where did you learn that grace?" she couldn't help asking.

Mrs. Lee smiled, as if remembering a funny story. "Our family always good Christian," she said. "And when I was little, I learn this from a nice missionary lady."

Missionary lady? Alice thought missionaries only went to really primitive lands, like Africa. She decided not to ask.

"You want to use fork, or chopsticks?" asked Yoon Jun.

"Fork," said Alice. The only time she'd ever used chopsticks was when she and her family had gone to a

Chinese restaurant, but she hadn't been able to get the hang of it.

Alice warily took a bite of the pancake. It was fluffy, almost eggy, and didn't taste like much.

"Here," said Mrs. Lee. "You can put some soy sauce on it." She handed Alice a tiny bowl that had soy sauce with pieces of green onion floating on top. Alice put some of that on, took another bite, and then tasted mostly salt.

"How you like it?" Mrs. Lee asked anxiously.

"Very good," said Alice. Of course she would rather have macaroni and cheese, but it wasn't too bad, really.

"Good," said Mrs. Lee, turning the dial of the griddle. "Now, we try another favorite Korean dish, *bulkoki*."

While the griddle heated, she spooned out some rice for everyone. This rice was sticky, and not as long-grained as the Minute Rice they had at home.

When the griddle started to smoke, Mrs. Lee brought out the bowl of meat — it *was* raw meat. She threw it and the bowls of mushrooms, spinach, and bean sprouts onto the hot surface. The meat, Alice noticed, was cut almost paper-thin, so it started turning from red to brown right away.

Merrily, Mrs. Lee stirred everything around as a cloud of smoke and steam rose from it. Alice smelled sizzling meat, ginger, and sesame. To her surprise, her mouth started to water.

Mrs. Lee ceremoniously lifted a clump of cooked meat and vegetables with her chopsticks and deposited it onto Alice's clean, white rice.

"And this," said Mrs. Lee, taking out some pink, suspicious-looking vegetable from a jar, "is Korea's national treasure, *kimchee*."

"What is it?" asked Alice, uneasily.

"Cabbage and spice, mainly," she said. "I just give you a small bit in case you not like it."

Alice looked down at the wilted leaf on her plate. This was the big deal they named that Korean camp in Brainerd after?

She tried the meat first because it looked safer. It was actually pretty good: soy-saucy and a little sweet. The vegetables had fried up crispy and delicious.

Alice looked over at Yoon Jun, who was shoveling food into his mouth as though he hadn't eaten in years. He made funny sucking noises as he ate — almost like oinking sounds. Alice shuddered slightly.

"Yoon Jun is telling me that he likes my cooking," said Mrs. Lee, catching Alice's gaze. Alice felt instantly embarrassed.

"In Korea," she went on, "you tell the cook you like her food by eating with lots of noise."

"Really? If I ate that way at home, my parents would kill me," Alice couldn't help saying.

Mrs. Lee smiled wisely. "Ah, Korean and American customs not always coincide. I am glad to learn more about American culture from you."

Alice was feeling more embarrassed by the minute. The Lees were obviously very poor, and here she was barging in and eating their food, and then acting as though Yoon Jun had bad manners.

The *kimchee* had been sitting forlornly on her plate for a while, so Alice finally lifted it up. It was mottled with angry red spices, and the pungent smell of vinegar tickled her nose. *Here goes nothing,* she thought, and she dropped the limp leaf into her mouth.

It was surprisingly crunchy, and spicy, and weird-tasting. But the more she chewed, the more she wanted to taste that sharp taste again, even though it stung her mouth. Soon, she had cleaned all the pieces off her plate.

"You like?" Mrs. Lee beamed.

"Yes," said Alice, holding her plate up for more. It wasn't exactly that the taste was good, it was more addictive.

"*Kimchee* is what makes Koreans so healthy," Mrs. Lee announced. "It is full of good things — hot peppers and garlic."

Garlic? thought Alice. She hated garlic. She hated it when she smelled it in Yoon Jun's lunch. Was he carrying *kimchee?*

Still, she couldn't help eating some more. It didn't taste all that garlicky to her. Mostly, it just tasted hot.

After dinner, Mrs. Lee served a warm, sweet tea that had grains of rice at the bottom. She also brought out the chocolates.

"Ah, chocolate," she said with relish. "This is one of the things I like best about America."

A little later, Mrs. Lee excused herself, and Alice saw her disappear into one of the small rooms down the hall. If that was the bathroom, the other must be the bedroom, she thought.

"Where is your room?" Alice inquired politely to Yoon Jun. He saw her looking down the hall.

"Over there." He pointed in the direction Alice was looking. "I share with my mother."

"What?" Alice said, sure she couldn't have heard right.

"I share room with my mother," he repeated.

Alice was astounded. "Don't you miss your privacy?"

"What for I need privacy?" he said. "We just sleep in there, and I like my mother. She don't snore or anything."

"But I'd go crazy if I had to sleep with my parents," said Alice. "Just knowing they were there."

Yoon Jun laughed. "You kidding? In Seoul, our whole family practically live in one room — me with all my cousins, and they snore and kick."

"Does everyone in Korea live like that?" Alice asked.

"Oh no," he said. "But Seoul very crowded. People have to grow gardens on top of buildings."

"Why would anyone want to live in Seoul?"

"My father had a job in a bank," Yoon Jun said,

and Alice saw his face turn sad. "Before he died, he had a very good job in a bank, and best jobs all in Seoul."

Alice wanted to ask him more about his father, and about why he and his mother came to the United States. But she suddenly realized how grateful she was that Yoon Jun and his mother weren't prying at her with a bunch of pesky questions about what it was like being adopted, did she have any idea what her Korean mother was like or why she gave her up — all those questions that rude people seemed to like to ask when they first met her.

Mrs. Lee returned to the table and sipped the rest of her rice tea thoughtfully. "You like *kimchee*, yes?" she asked Alice.

"Yes, I do," Alice answered sincerely.

Mrs. Lee broke into a smile. "Good," she said. "Then I will put some in a jar for you. Maybe mother and father would like to try, too."

"Oh, that's very nice of you," said Alice quickly. The Lees seemed so poor — she didn't want to take what little food they had. "But you don't have to do that. It was already so nice of you to share this dinner with me."

"If you like," Mrs. Lee said, smiling with satisfaction, "then perhaps mother and father will like, too." She excused herself from the table, and Alice could hear the clinking of a jar.

"Your mom is awfully nice," Alice said to Yoon Jun, low.

"Yes," Yoon Jun agreed. "She likes to give of herself. Now, you think this food okay to serve at school?"

"More than okay," Alice said. "Do you need me to get anything from the grocery store?"

"Oh no, don't worry," he said.

Mrs. Lee returned with a jar full of *kimchee*. "Now, you make sure to give mother and father a taste," she said with a laugh.

Chapter 27

❀ ❀ ❀

In some ways, Alice was almost sad to leave the apartment. Before, Mrs. Lee and Yoon Jun had seemed so foreign, but now, strangely, they seemed almost familiar.

She was thinking back to what Laura had asked: Did she have any memories of Korea? She didn't. Babies don't remember things. But she had read somewhere that people thought babies could hear things while still in their mothers' bellies.

Could that be possible? She didn't understand a single word of Korean, but when Yoon Jun and his mother were speaking that singing language to each other, Alice knew she had heard those sounds before. She *knew* it.

The few times Alice had even thought about Korea, she always fantasized that her mother was a beautiful Korean princess — if they had princesses in Korea — and that her father was a prince or something. Sometimes she imagined that her mother was a blue-eyed blonde who had to give Alice up because the royal family of her husband, the Korean king, objected, and one day she would wake up to find that the blonde genes had taken over.

That's what she would like best, she decided, to be able to blend in completely with her family. To be blonde like Mary. But as she thought this, she couldn't ignore the sounds of Korean words beating like far-off drums in her head.

At dinner the next night, Alice let everyone try the *kimchee*.

"What's this?" said her father. "Korean pickles?"

"Pickled cabbage," said Alice. "It's called *kimchee*. Mrs. Lee said it's one of Korea's national treasures."

Mrs. Larsen eyed the jar uneasily. She took a sniff. "My," she said. "It sure smells spicy."

"Looks ucky," concluded Mary.

"Now, don't call anything ucky until you've tried it," said Reverend Larsen. To set an example, he fished out a rather large piece of it and deposited it into his mouth, without smelling it or anything. He coughed once as he chewed.

"Mmm," he said, through his beard. "This is quite good."

He took another piece. Alice's mother sliced a small piece off of that and ate it. Her eyes grew wide as she did. "I was right," she said. "It *is* spicy."

"Here, Mare," Alice said to her little sister. She cut her a piece the size of a fingernail. "It's not as bad as it looks — it's interesting."

Mary looked up trustingly at her sister, and then ate the piece. She chewed and chewed and chewed, seemingly forever, then finally swallowed.

"Okay, Alice, it wasn't so bad. Can I have some ice cream now?"

Chapter 28

❀ ❀ ❀

International Day finally came, and Alice woke up with butterflies. So many things could go wrong, she thought.

Alice got to school early and met Minna and Laura there. Minna was wearing feathers in her hair.

"Nice feathers," Alice commented.

"I don't know about this," Minna grumbled. "After I do all the work on the report, look what Fred brings as food."

She thrust something that looked like a piece of leather at them. "This is dried meat — Indian pemmican," she said.

"Isn't pemmican supposed to be made of buffalo?" asked Laura.

"Sure looks like beef jerky to me," said Alice.

"It *is* beef jerky," said Minna. "I think he just bought it at the five and dime."

Alice suddenly thought about Yoon Jun. He had

refused all of her offers to help bring the food to school.

"I'd better go find Yoon Jun to see if he needs any help," she said, to slightly surprised looks from Minna and Laura. "After all, he's bringing all the food. Now, don't forget to stop by — the food is actually good."

Alice walked around the tables in the gym until she found the one that had been assigned to them. Yoon Jun was already there, unloading plastic containers of food.

"Wow," said Alice, looking at the two large shopping bags he carried. "This is a lot of food."

"We don't want nobody to go hungry," Yoon Jun reasoned.

Alice thought about the cramped apartment. This food must have cost a fortune.

Alice pulled out a ten-dollar bill, a pretty sizable chunk of her savings.

"Here," she said to Yoon Jun. "This food must have cost a lot."

"Well, I just work an extra shift," said Yoon Jun, making no move to take the money.

"Please take it," said Alice. "It'll make me feel better."

Yoon Jun looked at the bill, then shrugged. "Okay," he said, smiling.

Alice helped him unload the food. She cut up the pancakes into pieces the size of Bazooka bubble gum.

Mrs. Choquette had said the object was to give everyone a taste, not to feed everyone a meal. Alice did her best to cut up the limp *kimchee,* but she doubted that too many people would try it, anyway. It just looked too strange.

She hoped that Travis Jones's father wouldn't show up.

Alice checked the chart to see what number she and Yoon Jun were in the presentation order. "We're number five," she told Yoon Jun.

When the principal rang the bell, the kids sat themselves in front of the makeshift stage at the side of the gym. The parents sat behind them, on folding chairs. Alice couldn't see Laura, but she did see Minna's feathers sticking out from the crowd.

The reports were supposed to be ten to fifteen minutes long, but after the first few teams went, Alice knew that five or six minutes was going to be more the norm.

When it was their turn, Alice and Yoon Jun hauled up their posters: a map of Korea and pictures of the food they were serving. Under all the names of the food, Yoon Jun had carefully lettered in the Korean names. The characters looked a lot like the ones she saw in Chinese restaurants, Alice noted.

Alice read the report, while Yoon Jun juggled the posters. She felt vaguely as if they were on a game show. The report talked about Korea's land, history, and, of course, the food. It took at least a good fifteen minutes.

Alice was surprised to hear a roaring in her ears when they finished. Was she coming down with something? Did it have something to do with the acoustics in the gym?

"Bravo!" she heard her father yell.

People were clapping loudly. From the corner of her eye, Alice could see Mrs. Choquette smiling at them.

Alice grabbed Yoon Jun by the sleeve. He was looking at the stage floor. "C'mon," she whispered. "Take a bow — they liked us."

Alice bowed, and Yoon Jun bowed stiffly with her. Then they ran off the stage.

"Great job," said Troy when he came to their booth afterward.

"What's there to eat?" asked Laura.

"Didn't you listen to our presentation?" Alice said with mock indignation. "This is *kimchee,* Korea's national treasure, this is *pin dae duk,* Korean pancakes, and this is *bulkoki,* Korean stir fry."

"It looks great," said Troy. "I'll take a little of everything."

"Hmm," said Laura. She didn't look so adventurous. "I'll take some of the meat and some rice."

"Try some *kimchee* too," said Alice, pushing a dish toward her.

"Hmm," Laura said again, uncertainly.

110

"Here, I'll take a bit — see, it's good." Alice was glad to see Troy already munching on his.

Laura took a tiny bite, which was hard because *kimchee* is stringy. She finally had to use her hands to separate herself from the piece she was eating.

"This stuff is hot," she said, fanning her mouth and hopping up and down.

"Isn't it good?" said Alice.

"Yeah, it's pretty good," said Troy.

For the rest of the time, Alice tried to get everyone who stopped by to try some *kimchee*. She ended up eating a lot of it herself to demonstrate how good it was. When her mom and dad came by, they tried everything, and her father had an extra helping of *kimchee*.

"You guys did a great job," said Mrs. Larsen. "I sure learned a lot about Korean history."

Yoon Jun nodded happily.

"And your posters made me hungry," said Reverend Larsen. "Yoon Jun — your mom is a terrific cook. You should open a restaurant."

"Yoon Jun already works at Country Kitchen," Alice piped up. "He could steal all their trade secrets, like a jukebox at every table."

Yoon Jun suddenly looked alarmed. It was that same look he had given Alice and her friends that night they saw him at Country Kitchen. *What does he have to be scared about now?* she wondered. We are, after all, sort of friends.

111

"What do you do there?" asked Reverend Larsen gently.

"I—I not work there often," said Yoon Jun. "Sometimes I busboy." Alice noticed that he was giving her a funny look — almost as if he was mad.

"Are you mad at me?" Alice asked, when her parents were gone.

"No," said Yoon Jun. He still had a wild look in his eyes. "I afraid."

Mrs. Lee came out of the crowd to their booth. "I have had many good things to eat," she said happily. "Chocolate, even."

"That's good, Ma," said Yoon Jun. "Everyone love your cooking."

Alice glanced over at Yoon Jun. To her, it looked as though he was making a Herculean effort to conceal his fear from his mother. Alice didn't have the slightest idea why he was so scared, but now she was a little worried herself.

Chapter 29

❀ ❀ ❀

Alice couldn't believe that she was so worried about Yoon Jun Lee. But something she had done had scared him, and she wanted to find out what it was.

She finally got to talk to him at lunch. She was glad to see that Fred Jorich and his friends were sitting with him again.

"Hi, Yoon Jun," Alice said, sitting next to him. Yoon Jun looked surprised, but not mad.

"Hello," he said, and smiled.

Alice decided to get to the point. "Remember at International Day, when you said you were afraid — was it because of something I said?"

"Not really," he said. "I just have some problem with my job."

"What do you mean?"

He looked around warily. "You see," he said. "I not old enough to work, so I tell the man at the restaurant that I sixteen. I tell him all my paper in Korean, so I can't prove it, but he believe me — I big for my age."

"That doesn't seem so awful to me," said Alice.

"Not really," said Yoon Jun. "But there is law that say need to be sixteen to work. If the man find out, he fire me — and I need the job."

Talking to Yoon Jun made Alice feel bad. It made her realize that she had so much, yet people like Yoon Jun and Julie Graywolf seemed to work so hard for so *little*.

If I'd stayed in Korea, would I be poor, too? she wondered.

A wild look had reappeared in Yoon Jun's eyes. "Now, Al-ice," he said. "I know your father very good man, but I afraid he tell Mr. Johnson, my boss, about me. I know it wrong for me to lie about my age, but my mother sick, and we need the money to buy expensive medicine."

"Your mother is sick?" Alice was suddenly alarmed. "What's wrong?"

"She has problems with her insides," he said. "Has been that way for a while."

"Don't worry — I'm sure my dad won't tell," Alice said, although she wasn't sure about that at all. She hoped she would get to him in time.

"You know what, Yoon Jun, I'll talk to him just to make sure."

"Yes?" said Yoon Jun gratefully.

"Right away," said Alice.

* * *

114

Alice waited until after dinner, when she could catch her father alone in his study.

"Daddy?" she said tentatively.

Her father looked up from the book he was reading. "Yes, dear?" he said.

"Daddy, you know Yoon Jun Lee —" She didn't know how to begin.

"Yes, I know him," her father said, chuckling.

"Well, his mother is sick, so —"

"Mrs. Lee is sick?" Reverend Larsen sat up with concern. "Does she need a doctor?"

"She's been sick for a while," said Alice. She wasn't explaining this very well. "What I meant to tell you is that Yoon Jun needs the money from his job to pay for her medication, so please don't tell his boss at Country Kitchen that he's not sixteen."

"Oh. Frankly, I'd forgotten about that," he said, to Alice's dismay. "But you know, I was thinking that he ought not to be working there — child labor laws are meant to protect the children."

"Oh, Daddy," said Alice, horrified. "I'm here because Yoon Jun asked me to ask you not to tell — especially after I blabbed like that at International Day."

"Alice, it's good that you told me," her father said. "There must be a better way for Yoon Jun to help his mother, and maybe it would be good for them to look into insurance or something like that."

All Alice could think of was how disappointed Yoon Jun was going to be when he found out that she'd made a royal mess of things.

"Do you know anything about his mother's illness?" Reverend Larsen asked gently.

"No," said Alice. She could feel her face falling.

"Now Alice," he said. "You know that it's practically my duty to let the fellow at Country Kitchen know about his employee. I do think that later on, Yoon Jun will thank you for being such a friend."

Such a friend! Alice sighed. This experience with her will probably sour Yoon Jun on the idea of making friends at Bainer at all.

Chapter 30

❀ ❀ ❀

For the next few days, Alice did her best to avoid Yoon Jun. He would sometimes wave or briefly smile at her at lunch, and she would just wave back and then run off someplace with Minna and Laura. She knew it was cowardly, but she didn't want to hear how he'd lost his job and how his mother was going without medicine.

"I'm sorry you're so upset about this," said Laura. They were taking refuge in the girls' bathroom.

"If he gets fired, I'll feel like it's all my fault," Alice said miserably.

"I like your dad and all," said Minna, "but it must be tough on you that he's a minister — he gets into things the way other dads wouldn't. You know, like if there's a sin involved, he has to do something about it."

"You're right, Minna," said Alice. "When I don't agree with him, he's always on the Christian side, which *has* to be right. Sometimes, he even reminds me that if not for 'Christian kindness,' I wouldn't be here.

It makes me feel like I must have done something really bad when I was young, and that's why they sent me out of Korea!"

Alice felt choked up. She used to avoid bringing up the subject of her adoption, but now in a funny way it felt good, almost like taking her aching feet out of tight shoes.

"Oh Alice," said Laura. "You were a little itty bitty baby then — 'innocent as a newborn babe' and all that."

"Maybe my Korean parents were bad, then."

"I doubt it," said Minna loyally, "or you wouldn't have turned out the way you did."

Alice gave her friends a hug. *Thank goodness for friends,* she thought.

Chapter 31

❋ ❋ ❋

The next day, Alice and Minna came to school extra early to put up some pep signs for the upcoming hockey season. Alice was excited because Troy had done really well in hockey camp last summer — she read this in an article in the *Bainer Bugle* by its new sports columnist, Peter Kemp — and he was expected to be one of the star players on the Junior High lineup this winter.

The cheerleaders had painted a big sign that said BAINER JR HIGH WILL TAKE THE ICE in Bainer-blue tempera paint, and Alice and Minna had volunteered to hang it in the cafeteria in the morning before everyone got to school.

"It's sort of weird being here when no one's around, isn't it?" said Minna, as they listened to their own footsteps clattering in the empty hall. It was still dark outside.

"Let's tiptoe," suggested Alice. "I don't want to

give the janitor a heart attack — and besides, I'm a little scared."

"Okay," said Minna, and they crept toward the cafeteria like spies.

Someone was in there, bending over one of the tables. At first Alice thought it was the janitor, but then she realized that the person, though big, was still a kid.

It was Travis Jones.

He looked at them, and then gave a sort of maniacal laugh and ran away.

Minna had a hand to her heart. "I don't like the idea of us being alone in the building with *him*," she squeaked.

Alice pulled the huge cafeteria doors shut until they clicked. "I think these are locked. Anyway, if they're not, at least he can't sneak up on us."

The two girls dragged out the ladder that the janitor had left for them.

As they passed the table where Travis Jones had been, Alice looked down and saw, in pencil, "Alice Larsen -n- Yoon Jun Lee Together 4-ever" in a half-drawn heart.

"Ooh!" Alice stamped her foot and dropped the sign. Minna looked over at her, confused.

"Travis Jones was the one who did that graffiti!" Alice shouted, not scared at all anymore. Who could be afraid of such a cowardly jerk?

"Uh-oh," said Minna. "And after we scared the pants off poor Yoon Jun Lee."

"I know." Alice sat on the table and put her chin in her hands. Minna sat next to her.

"I still have to apologize for my father's telling the Country Kitchen man," Alice said. "And now how am I going to explain this? I was so mean to him."

"First things first," Minna said logically. She glanced out the cafeteria window. "We'd better get the sign up."

Reluctantly, Alice agreed. She helped Minna tape up the sign, but her mind was thinking a jillion other things. How could she have been so awful to Yoon Jun?

* * *

Alice thankfully got through the day without encountering Yoon Jun. Minna had said she would help Alice figure out what to do.

After practice, the two girls trotted out into the cold and dark. The stars weren't out yet, but three quarters of a moon shone balefully.

"Brrr," said Minna. "It's getting cold! Let's dash to Country Kitchen and get a Coke."

The girls half walked, half ran toward the restaurant. They were thankful to see the sign flickering orange on the other side of the highway.

"No cars," said Minna, looking over her shoulder. She started to shiver harder in the wind. "Let's go!"

They started across the road, but suddenly Alice saw a big figure in front of them. He was waving his arms and yelling "Wait!" The next thing she knew, the person had practically flown across the highway and knocked both of them down.

Alice heard a car zoom by and screech to a halt, then she heard Minna crying. What was happening? Was this guy a kidnapper? Her ankle had twisted under her so she couldn't run.

"Are you okay?"

Alice looked up and was surprised to see Yoon Jun Lee.

"My ankle," she said. "What happened?"

Yoon Jun pointed to a car that had come peacefully to rest in the culvert by the side of the road. "He almost run you down," said Yoon Jun.

Alice squinted. Some people from Country Kitchen were now running across the road to them. She couldn't understand it — the car was pointing the wrong way.

"Alice," Minna whimpered in the dark, "are you all right?"

"I'm okay," Alice said, even though her ankle was killing her. This was all too strange. Why had she been tackled by Yoon Jun Lee?

Alice saw the flashing lights of a police car, and an ambulance.

Chapter 32

❀ ❀ ❀

"Okay, let me get this straight," said Laura. She and Minna were sitting next to Alice on her bed. Alice's ankle was propped up on a bag of ice.

"You and Minna were crossing the highway to Country Kitchen, and you didn't see that car?"

"It came up the wrong way," explained Minna. "The guy was drunk."

"And Yoon Jun Lee saved you?"

"Yeah," said Alice. "He was coming back from returning his uniform because he had been fired — thanks to my dad — and he saw the car and knocked us out of the way."

Laura jotted a few things in her notebook. "This is definitely front-page news," she said. "A hero in our midst."

"He is," said Minna. "He could've been killed doing what he did."

"Have you talked to him?" Laura asked.

"I said hi to him in school today," said Minna.

"I haven't talked to him at all," groaned Alice. "Can you imagine: he's fired from his job because of my dad, I yell at him about this graffiti when it's really Travis Jones — and then after all that, he saves our lives! I feel like such a jerk."

"Don't be so hard on yourself," said Laura. "When are you coming back to school?"

"Friday," said Alice. "I have to go get my crutches tomorrow."

The doorbell sounded downstairs.

"Hi, gals." It was Troy. He had a bunch of carnations in his hand.

"Hi, Troy," the three girls chorused. Minna ran downstairs to get a vase and water.

"How're you feeling, Alice?"

"Okay." She felt ridiculous, with her foot sticking out all purple and swollen.

"We've got to get home, now," said Minna, after she'd arranged the flowers prettily on Alice's dresser.

"Oh, stay," said Alice, but she knew they wouldn't.

"No way, we've got a ton of homework, don't we, Laura?"

"Yep, and I've got to get going on this hero story. Thanks for the details, Alice."

The two girls left in a clatter.

"I guess we're not going to go skiing anytime soon, huh?" said Troy, sitting gently on the bed.

"I guess," said Alice.

The doorbell sounded again.

"Laura and Minna are such space cadets," said Alice. "Laura probably forgot her notebook — she always does."

"Al-ice?" said a familiar voice.

Chapter 33

❀ ❀ ❀

Yoon Jun Lee stood in Alice's bedroom door. He looked around her room as if he were entering a huge cave. He nodded politely to Troy, after Alice motioned him in.

"Hi, Yoon Jun," she said, trying to get over her surprise. "Yoon Jun Lee, this is Troy Hill."

"Hi there," said Troy. "You're a really brave guy, you know."

Yoon Jun looked at the floor. He was smiling. "Not so brave," he said. "It nothing. I want to know how you do, Alice."

"Oh, better," she said. "I'll be back in school Friday. My ankle's only sprained."

"You know, Yoon Jun," said Troy, "you might want to think about going out for football next year. You'd make a great defensive player." Alice could see real admiration in his eyes.

"Foot-ball?" said Yoon Jun.

"Yeah," said Troy, pretending to cradle a ball and rush for a touchdown. "You know."

Yoon Jun smiled. Alice wasn't sure if he got it, but she was happy that he and Troy seemed to be getting along.

"We can talk more about it when the season starts," said Troy. He looked at his watch.

"Gosh," he said. "I'd better get to the arena so I can finish the *hockey* season." He waved goodbye to Alice and Yoon Jun, and then he was out the door.

Alice felt a heavy silence settle on them after the last noise of Troy's feet died away.

"This a very nice room," Yoon Jun said.

"Thanks," said Alice. Yoon Jun was still Yoon Jun, she thought. Pudgy, weird accent. But he had also saved her life — even after she'd been so awful to him.

"Yoon Jun, I'm sorry," she said suddenly, and she clutched her bedspread for support.

"What for sorry?" asked Yoon Jun gently.

Alice smoothed the bedspread with her hands. "For being mean to you at lunch, for having my dad getting you fired from your job."

Yoon Jun's eyes had a look that seemed to Alice to be much too old for a seventh-grader.

"What I care about job?" he said lightly. "What I care about is mother."

"What are you going to do now?"

Yoon Jun smiled. "Your father say he will take care

127

of mother's medicine with — what is word? — insurance. And what is left over he said the church can give us."

"Really?" said Alice. Her father was more resourceful than she thought.

"I very grateful to you and your father," Yoon Jun said.

"Well, I am sorry about telling you to quit drawing the hearts on the cafeteria tables — I thought it was you, but it was someone else."

"Why you keep saying sorry?" Yoon Jun looked a little annoyed. "Your father and mother are good people, so I figure you okay. No need to say sorry for nothing."

They grew quiet again.

"Yoon Jun, can I ask you something?" Alice said tentatively.

He nodded.

"Why did you and your mother leave Korea?"

Yoon Jun stared at her for a second. He took off his glasses and stared at them. He cleared his throat.

"I love Korea very much," he said. "But when my father die, it change many things, so my mother and I need to change, also. We come here, I suppose, for better life. In some ways, like you come here for better life."

Alice's chest tightened. "But I didn't come here because I wanted to. My Korean parents gave me up — they abandoned me."

"Al-ice," he said. "They not give you up because they not want you, because they not love you. For some babies, there is no life in Korea, and is much better to grow up somewhere else. The parents suffer so child can have better life."

She did have a good life, and she knew it. But what ever happened to the lady who gave birth to her? Would she ever be able to tell her how happy she was? She had no idea what kind of life she had left behind, and it felt like a big gaping hole in her memory.

Maybe one day, she thought, *the people at the adoption agency could help me find my Korean parents so I could write to them and tell them I'm okay, that I'm happy. Maybe Yoon Jun could act as a translator.*

"You know, Yoon Jun," she said. "I'm glad you moved here."

"Well, I very glad you glad," said Yoon Jun.

Chapter 34

❀ ❀ ❀

The next day, Alice got her crutches. She was trying them out when the doorbell rang.

"I'll get it, Mom," she yelled. "I need the practice." She hobbled to the door and opened it.

Outside in the bright afternoon sun stood Dusty Prince and Julie Graywolf.

"Wow," said Alice with surprise. "C'mon in — that is, if I can figure out how to put these crutches in reverse."

Julie and Dusty followed her into her house, up the stairs, and into her room.

"How'd you get out of cheerleading practice?" Alice asked Dusty.

"I walked," she said, and then grinned. It was the friendliest Alice had seen her in ages. Julie hung back a little, looking around the way Yoon Jun did when he was here.

"You know," Dusty continued, "when I heard

about what happened to you and Minna, I realized how sad I'd be if you guys were gone."

"Oh, Dusty," Alice said. She still had visions of Dusty running across the school lawn. She had thought for sure that Dusty would never want to be friends with her and Laura and Minna again.

"I realized how silly it was to hold a grudge," Dusty said. "Why should I demand that you guys be perfect when no one is — I'm certainly not."

"I can see why you'd be mad: we were pretty cowardly in the face of Travis Jones," Alice admitted.

"Well, I heard about your encounter with Travis's father at the dance," said Dusty. "So I'm sure you have a better understanding of what it feels like."

"And where Travis gets it from," Julie added sadly. Alice nodded.

"You know," said Dusty, "I really have to hand it to that Japanese kid —"

"He's Korean," Alice corrected. "Like me."

"Korean," said Dusty. "He's really something — pushing you guys out of the path of the car like that."

"He is," Alice agreed. "You know, Julie, I'd like you to meet him. He's really nice — just like you."

In the afternoon light, Julie's face looked less tough. Alice thought she looked pretty, especially the way her dark eyes were so striking. "I'd like to meet him," she said. "Maybe we can all do something some time."

"Yeah," agreed Dusty. "We can all go horseback riding."

"That'd be great," said Alice excitedly. "Minna would just die."

"Okay," said Dusty. "After your foot gets better, we'll go."

"Sounds good to me," agreed Julie.

Chapter 35

❀ ❀ ❀

Alice's world was in place again. It was hard to get around at school, but she had enough friends handy to help her with stairs and the like, and it was kind of fun to be the center of attention.

Yoon Jun didn't sit alone at lunch anymore. He ate with Fred Jorich and his friends every day, and sometimes Troy and some other football players joined him. Once in a while, Alice even sat with him, "to get some Korean goodies" — even though Mrs. Lee was showing her mother how to make them herself.

And every few weeks or so, she and Yoon Jun would sit by the bust of Noah Webster in the library and learn more about Korea. He was even teaching her some Korean, and Alice had to admit that the Korean language sounded pretty neat. It made Alice think that maybe her father was right: It *is* a good idea to learn about other cultures.

Today was one of those language lesson days.

"*Chingu*," said Yoon Jun, as they sat at their usual table, "is the Korean word for friend."

"Chin-goo," Alice repeated. "Did I say it right?"

"You said it very nice," said Yoon Jun.